# Rogue World

# Rogue World

F. O. Hill

Village Books
Bellingham, Washington

Village Books
1200 11th St, Bellingham, WA 98225
(360) 671-2626
www.villagebooks.com

Library of Congress Control Number 2016906287
ISBN 9780692692417

Printed in the United States of America

To the storiers who show us
who we were, are, and can be.

# Contents

*Rogue World*

Rogue World
F.O. Hill

*We have a long history, and each of your ancestors has a story, but some are more powerful than others. This is one of them, but it has never been told outside the clan. It goes back a long, long way, to a time when we came to be who we are today. It is the story of one boy who stumbled into manhood, a boy who failed to follow the rules, and who saved our people. It begins in darkness before time and grows now in this, the land of imagination.*

Chapter One

# Hunger

They came in the night while Kai slept. He had been left alone in the underground refuge for three days without food, and they attacked the village in the darkest hour while he wrestled through a confusing barrage of dreams that slowed to one, clear image of a young woman.

In the dream he stands alone looking out over a wide, open space, larger that any place he had ever seen. The bright sky seemed to go on forever, and a strong wind pushed against him, whipping the tips of the light brown grass that then became suddenly lazy and gentle as the wind moved away.

The air was cold, clear, and so sharply fresh that he did not care if it chilled and intimidated him in this vast expanse of openness. There was not a tree in sight. He felt his spirit rise and tingle. This place was so unlike any he knew that he felt it must be more than a simple dream.

Although he wanted to move, to explore this place, Kai was rooted to the ground, as if a great weight were upon him. There was silence, a dead silence now that the wind had passed, and it grew deeper and more relaxing, lulling him until suddenly, for no reason, his mind cleared and a powerful fear hit him full force.

His hands began to shake as he twisted in his place, his knees instinctively flexing to let him sink toward the grass for what little cover it could offer. As far as he could see, the land sloped away, but something was moving, off there, in the distance.

He tried to bring it into focus, but it was too far off to see clearly. However, from the way it moved, he knew it was a person walking toward him across the wide expanse, walking straight toward his hiding place, casually.

He looked around; there was nowhere to go, no sign of cover, and there was no one else as far as he could see, yet Kai had that fear running up his backbone as certainly as he breathed. He wanted to escape, but he was too heavy. He could not move.

So he pulled together what courage he could find and turned instead to face the one approaching. He rose to his full height, but at 15 that was not too intimidating and it made the person coming seem to grow, too. His loose shirt stretched against his back tightly as he flexed, and his hand dropped to the bone handle of his knife, lightly brushing his right thigh. His knuckles tensed around the familiar grip. He slowed his breathing, taking in the cold air, and his heart began to slow as well. He waited for whatever was coming.

He could not make out the features on the face as it bobbed above the slight curves of the grass between them; they were vague and hazy still, but he could tell that it was a woman. Kai relaxed as she came closer. She was smiling. She grew steadily as she came, and as she climbed the small rise in the land toward him, she began to raise her arm, as if holding something out for him. Smiling, she lurched forward to the ground.

He dropped, too, his knife out. There was only the sound of the breeze in the grass. When he was sure that no one else was moving within the field of his vision, he crawled toward her, slowly, deliberately, methodically. Free from the crushing weight of a few moments before, he rose and hunched over and seemed to soar the short distance between them. As he knelt near her motionless body, he noticed a small, neat hole—burned black around the edges—in the back of her leather jacket. There was little blood. Gently, he rolled her over, looking around him again as he did. He saw no one.

She was pretty—dark, long hair and high, well defined cheekbones like his sisters'. Her eyes began to glaze over as he watched, and a small bloody bubble grew from her perfect nose. As he eased her head back down onto the ground, her eyes began to lose their glassy quality, and she made an effort to speak. All that came from her quivering lips was "the lights." Before he could ask, she turned her eyes toward his hand. He offered it. With great pain, she poured heavy, dark soil into his opened palm. Her hand fell and as she slipped away Kai felt an uncontrollable pang of grief for this stranger.

Kai awoke sweating, and as he rolled over onto his stomach to rise, he found that his aching fist was clinched tightly, almost against his will. It was numb and unresponsive; he had to force it open with his free hand, and in it he found dirt. Before he could decipher this curious fact, the first sounds of the attack shattered the night silence. There was no discernible rhythm to the increasingly intense throbs that were short and unusual and shook the building. Then one came louder than the rest. Dust and small chunks of debris showered on him as stone, mortar and wood gave way to the dry, intense pulse of their attack.

Later, he would learn that there had been no warning. Even the sentries stood dumbfounded at first. They had neither heard nor seen a thing until the first alarm came from behind them, deep in the village. The raiders emerged silently out of the dark to move methodically through the loose scattering of homes, dealing quickly and efficiently with any spontaneous, pitiful resistance that was offered. Their passing caused the ground to shake near Kai's sanctuary.

Instinctively, Kai rolled to his left, his arms rising to cover his head. A rock—the size of his head and jagged—dropped in a shower of debris onto his sleeping mat, one sharp edge scraping his shoulder and side before he could finish his roll. This brought him fully awake and he scampered toward the ladder and door leading out of the underground room, scrambling frantically on his hands and knees. As his senses were returned he probed the darkness ahead of him for any flicker of light. The screams from above and the smell of burning matter were enough to tell him that evil had arrived.

His grandfather's stories popped into his head, coming to life. He remembered the fear from those nights as a child when his grandfather's voice changed and he began to speak about the raiders and the death and losses that came with them. As he grew up, he began to believe that they were just stories used just to frighten kids to keep them under control, but now, searching for an explanation for the terror he felt in his churning stomach as the screams intensified above, he wasn't so sure.

Where he had hoped to find the ladder, he found instead a pile of broken and unrecognizable edges. Groping for footing in the dark, he scrambled up the steep, loose incline, shocked, then angered, that such a sacred place could be the target of so devastating an attack. He cursed them loudly, his puny voice giving him courage to push harder, climb faster. The anger grew large in his mind, and he wished for a fleeting moment that there was no rule against weapons and bad thoughts in sacred places. He pictured himself erupting into the night to stop the attack and make the raiders pay. But these thoughts were as swift as his motions to reach the door he hoped still existed, and they reversed as often as his direction: first anger and then fear as he slid backwards into the dark as loose gravel and dirt gave way and his fingers dug for a hold.

It took agonizing minutes for him to find where the door had been, in its place, rubble. He worked frantically at the left margin of the pile. The roof and door frame had collapsed, so the only space available to move stones he found on that side where he could simply roll them, sometimes pivoting the larger ones, off into the dark chamber below where they created small avalanches, and then were quiet.

His throat grew hot and dusty, but he persisted, despite his wasted condition, his sapped strength, and the pain in his shoulder. Sweat began to flow down his spine as he heaved and grunted. Hunger no longer concerned him. Instead, brief bright images of his mother, his two sisters, and his young brother. These images did not allow him to slow or rest. He forced them away with each thrust against a stone, turning the energy from each physical exertion into a mental victory, turning each fresh image into another ounce of strength, another ounce of resolve. But the tears were as close as the next twinge of frustration.

Every moment seemed to collapse back upon itself, just as the pile would seem to increase as he tore rocks from it only to have others fall into their places. When his energy and breath were almost gone, his spirit flickered. Then he would catch a faint fan of firelight from outside, and the thought of his village burning spurred him to new effort. He heard shouting nearby and shouted back but there was no reply.

But he made slow progress. When he had a hole the size of his head, he could see that the home across the way was on fire, and here and there shapes danced through the eerie light of his narrow field of vision. He thrust his head farther, and twisted his lean shoulders trying to find room for a passage. It was not there and he tore another jagged gash in his wounded shoulder trying to retreat. Although he could feel no pain, he could feel his hand growing sticky with blood as he turned back to his work.

There was a shout, and he watched the roof on the burning home collapse into a shower of sparks. He froze. He had seen this before. No, something like it. But this was only a momentary illusion, so he stooped again to devote his passing strength to one large rock that must have been the anchor for the doorframe. Once removed, he might be free.

It would not budge, but as he crumbled against it to blow and gather his nerve for another try, he noticed a small crack in the mortar at its base. His excited fingers probed for a weakness there. They found mortar caked with age that came away in great gritty handfuls. His hope rose.

Between the large rock and the one next to it he made an opening large enough for a handhold. As he leaned to find the right level for leverage, bear hugging the cold stone, his left hand groped farther into the opening that widened beyond his sight. His fingers slid across a flat, smooth, hard surface. It turned as he put pressure upon it. The rock did not. It was angular; the rock was contoured. He tried to force it out to make more room for the rock to pivot, but it became wedged between the foundation stone and its neighbor, and he could not pry it out in his direction. There was another shout outside and he returned with newfound strength and determination to the loose debris on the other side of the stone.

Men were digging from the outside; he could hear their excited jabber and their tools. As he reached his small opening he could see legs and hear the men rolling away stones. He shouted. They answered. In a few moments, working from both sides, they had an opening large enough for Kai to squeeze through. He stepped into the chilled, smoky night air. Dawn was approaching. Around him, there was chaos.

Once he was freed, the others left him alone as they

rushed toward another fire at the far end of the village. The devastation was not as extensive as he had expected. He wandered vaguely in the same direction the others had taken, the sudden end of exertions slowly turning his taut muscles into rubber.

Only three homes had been set ablaze—the one he had first seen and now two more on the far perimeter. The close one was almost completely burnt; the others were raising a bright aura over the village. As he moved toward it, the terrible, obvious logic of the attack slowly dawned upon him. The first fire was in the center, the last on the edge. He quickened his pace. They had chosen two points widely separated, one designed to draw defense, the other far enough away to separate the village's forces for their retreat. Kai's house was directly in-between.

Kai found his mother slumped in a corner, his brother clutched in her stunned, thoughtless arms. She stared at the doorway, even as Kai blocked it from her view with his body. A dark blue bruise was beginning to appear from the red flush on her right cheek. She did not blink or move or indicate that she knew he was present, even though he stooped to stroke her cheek.

"Mom. Mom, look at me." She flinched when he pried his younger brother free, wild-eyed in his fear, but he could not get her to stand. It was several minutes later that he found her left arm was broken in two places. It was not until later still that her eyes grew glassy, and that she let her grief bring her back. It was at that moment Kai realized his two sisters were missing.

By dawn the fires had burned themselves out. Only frail columns of smoke remained to remind each person of the night. Like Kai's mother, they were numb and had to look to the smoke wisps to verify that something awful and significant had happened, although sometimes trying to convince themselves that the raid had been a bad dream sparked by childhood stories of evil, faceless monsters that stalked the dark. "So little happens here," they would think, "and our days are like one another. How should one suddenly bring this . . . this . . .?" And it was true. For all time it seemed, their village had remained the same: sheltered, tranquil, secure. It would not be like that again for a long, long time.

Each generation heard the stories, and each called them myth, or legend, or fairy tale. Like the smoke ascending from the destroyed homes, they became the wisps of folklore. But there would be the occasional generation—now Kai's included—that would awake to a gray dawn as the smoke of destruction rose quietly, and think of the stories, and turn their thoughts into action as they—without signal or call—would slowly converge upon the center of their village as if gravity drew them there.

By the time Kai arrived after turning the care of his mother and brother over to his aunt, the village had gathered outside the ruin of the building Kai had escaped only a short time earlier. They stood in small groups, talking in subdued tones, or alone, looking at the rubble and collapse of the smoldering house near them. No single person stepped forward to unify them into one unit, or call them to action. Kai knew it would take time and deliberation for them to act. He knew that they would wait a bit longer, for the smaller meeting when the old men would discuss their ideas and then an action would be determined. He knew, as well, the outcome, both of the meeting and the action. They all knew. He wanted to scream at them, push them on and get them going, even if failure was the end result.

As he spoke with his boyhood friends in a small group, barely enduring their unspoken pity at his loss, his uncle appeared at the hole Kai had crawled through only a brief time before. The old man's stiff and brittle frame required that he exit on his belly, wiggling from side to side and using his elbows to draw himself forward. Before Kai could jump to assist him, however, his uncle rose to his knees, and then his feet, to dust himself off and recollect his full stature and dignity. He had presented a humorous spectacle, and at any other time he would have laughed with his people at his own lizard-like image. It raised a slight chuckle in him even now, but he quickly squelched it. Although age afforded him the distance to be amused, his responsibilities and his heart demanded his stern concentration. Like his life, these moments of loss were no easy thing, and he no simple man.

"It's badly damaged, but the interior chamber is intact." There was a murmur through the crowd, which had drawn tightly around old Luther as he spoke. Some looked to him with unblinking eyes, a few of which gleamed with hatred for the attackers, others with tears. Their actions varied but all listened intently, fixing this new information into their minds fanning their hopes for revenge, or a future.

"We can remove the collapsed roof, and two of the upper

crumbled walls. We should be able to rebuild . . .." His words tapered off into less than a firm assertion. It was not intended as a question. It was only that he felt his fatigue, his age suddenly. Building should be the work of younger minds and hands. With that thought, he looked to Kai, spotting him in the middle of the crowd. His face was firm and set, and it revealed his mind. "We must be thankful that young Kai was fortunate enough to escape."

"But what about my sisters?" Kai's impatience lurked just below the surface of his rigid young face. He was not accusing, not challenging, but simply directing the village's attention away from rocks and rubble to bone and flesh that needed saving, and soon. His sisters were being dragged away as they stood around chatting.

"Go. Prepare yourselves. The elders will meet at mid-day. Bring food, and water. We have some grave decisions to make." Before Kai could respond, his uncle stepped into the dispersing crowd and was lost in the crush.

He found him later with his mother, stroking her hair and whispering words of consolation. As he spoke, her eyelids drooped, fluttered, then closed. Kai watched in wonder as her facial muscles relaxed and she became young again— bright and carefree in her deep sleep.

Now, the similarities between her face and that of the young boy asleep on the mat beside her were strikingly apparent. Kai's heart burned as his throat constricted, and his love for his family welled up to cloud his vision. He had not seen his mother so flushed and full of life, so innocent, as now, in one of her darkest times.

Although he had not recognized it, since it came so slowly

upon her, she had aged. Since his father's death from the disease, she had carried the heavy duty of her children. True, they did not go without food or shelter. They worked hard to survive, and the community took care of its own. If anyone ate, they all ate, and if anyone suffered, they all suffered. But she had been burdened with concern. She had to think of her children and their futures, even though old Luther came to help her. Also, she had to worry about the disease that had taken her man, the disease that both Kai and his uncle knew had hold of her, too. The signs of its wasting effects had appeared only recently, but they were unmistakable and once the disease came there was no cure. This, too, had compounded her concern for her children. But, this is how we are, Kai thought. We care for each other, and the tears came then at the thought of his mother's compassion, and at the thought of losing her. Even short absences with visits to one of the other villages were painful, but this long, this endless missing? And now, his sisters were lost, too.

He turned to Luther, who was watching him closely. "We must go for them, now."

"Of course." The old man rose slowly. A night without sleep was a terrible thing, he thought. "Of course we will. There's nothing else to do. We would be less than ourselves if we didn't, but the results will be the same and we must prepare for that." There was an unfathomable depth to the despair behind the old man's words, and Kai was silenced for a moment as he pondered its significance. Then he felt the urge to move, to act, return with new urgency. How could his uncle and the others tolerate this delay when the obvious path was open?

14

"Uncle, the longer we wait, the more time they have to get away, the better prepared they will be. We should follow them right now, immediately, and catch them in the forest."

"Kai. They are already prepared for our coming. It is in their nature to be prepared. Remember, they planned this attack. They will have planned their escape as well." He let the obvious sink in before he continued. That's how uncles talked, in circles sometimes. It frustrated Kai and added to his need for action. "We need to prepare. We need to send runners to the people in the west and south, to see if they have been hit, too, and to gather as many men as possible. Then, we need to make ourselves ready, because many of us will not return."

Kai knew the truth of what he said, but it didn't help. "They will have reached the mountains by then."

"It cannot be helped. They are ahead of us and they will remain ahead of us. So, we must do what we must do, and make ready to die if it is to be so. Remember. You are still a boy. Your initiation is still incomplete, so do not slow us down with idle demands and do not challenge the wisdom of those who have lived longer and seen more."

From his uncle, a man of soft words and gracious smiles, this came as a stinging criticism and Kai was silenced by it, although the old man's voice never rose above a whisper, a singsong to soothe his sister-in-law's sleep. So this is author-ity, thought Kai. His uncle's words and the power of his speaking them went deeply into him, calling for him to con-trol his racing thoughts, but also to a renewed conviction. It wasn't his fault the initiation, that old relic of the past, hadn't been completed. And they were his sisters.

"I will return after the meeting to tell you when, and where. For now, look to your mother, begin your leave-taking. You will come with us as a runner to bring home reports of our movements." He did not leave the silent home, however, without first placing a soft, but firm, hand on Kai's shoulder, and then he touched, lightly, the center of the boy's forehead with the tips of the first two fingers of his left hand. Kai felt the power, a surging, warm sensation running the full length of his spine. Then it passed, and in the old man's eyes there remained a sparkle and gleam beyond age, grief, wisdom. "Eat something, and take care of your wounds."

Chapter Two
# Renegade

Kai sat on a bench just outside the door of his home. The sky was clear, but the light from above seemed so remote that it did not warm him, or his chilled thoughts. When he felt as if he would shiver, he worked harder, faster, honing his knife's edge. The increase in activity, however, carried with it no increase in the intensity of the noises he made. His mother and brother needed their sleep. It was the only drug they knew, the only painkiller except the nearness of family and clan. But perhaps there is more, he thought, as he paused in his work to remember the slight, powerful touch of his uncle.

Out of the corner of his eye, he watched his oldest friend, Shawn, approach cautiously, at first, and then more boldly. There was hesitancy in his coming, a halting quality to his motion accompanied by a great deal of looking around. Then his resolve took control and he bore down upon the sitting boy with the force of a storm, blocking out the light momentarily with his bulk.

"I'm on my way to the meeting. I heard that two are wounded—your mother and Lon, Pel's brother. He may not live. There are other people with small wounds." He paused and looked off to the farthest edge of the village. "We will make them pay. And we will get your sisters back."

He spoke with conviction and too much feigned authority for Kai's tastes. Great, he thought, now Shawn's going to rub it in, too. Kai bristled at the thought. The whole village knew what was going to happen. Shawn only repeated common knowledge as if he had decided matters himself. But Kai held his tongue. It was not his place to call out his friend, and they were still friends despite their ages and positions. Shawn was only slightly older but he had passed his initiation already and now wore the mark of his new manhood like a cloak about him, full of show and pretense. But Kai understood his visit. His mere presence spoke for him. He felt Kai's pain, but would not reveal his concern, because this was his idea of weakness and despite, or perhaps because of, his size Shawn never wanted to appear weak.

Kai looked him over carefully. They were nearly the same age, true, but Shawn was much larger and had matured, physically, before Kai and the others. He had always been larger than all the other boys of their generation, but now, his baby fat gone, his physique had begun to take on the angular shapes of a wrestler. He was taller, broader, more thickly set than Kai, who was remarkable in his average qualities. Slim, taller than some shorter than others, he liked to think of himself as light and fast. A runner rather than a wrestler. His long brown hair flowed behind him when he ran races, which he usually won, or when they swam.

But, as he looked to Shawn's waist and the knife that hung, like his own, from the rawhide belt, he began to doubt his own abilities. He felt with force the very nature of his boyhood. His baby fat had dissolved into contours, sloping shoulders, thin arms and legs. The journey into the mountains and the battle were, indeed, for men like Shawn. Besides, he would not decide anything. Others would and he'd have to follow along when he should be racing ahead, closing the distance between raider and retribution.

"Let me know what is decided."

"I will come straight back, and Kai, I am sorry." He spun quickly around and hurried away. Kai felt the sincerity in his coming, as well as the sense of personal purpose in his departure. That is Shawn; he has always been big, even clumsy at times, but always sincere, and always big-hearted.

He turned back to sharpening his knife. He had already restrung his bow and looked to his arrows, sighting down each familiar shaft while spinning it, testing feathers and points. His journey clothes of thick leather to resist the short brush along the trails, extra footwear, amulets and small rations of food were tied into a neat bundle at his feet. He was ready to go and time rested heavily upon him. He would have to wait a long while as they debated the obvious, and then he would have to convince them to let him bring his weapons. This would also take precious time. He looked at Shawn's back as he disappeared around the corner.

He wondered how much Shawn had seen during his initiation. The images Kai packed with him from the first part of his were frightening, and he did not know what to do with them because when they came back in his head, he felt dread and fear climb up his spine. These were feelings he'd rather not take with him on the chase.

There was the dream of the dead girl that he had not had

time to share with anyone. But there was also the thing of the fire that he and his uncle saw together. He was still trying to untangle the meaning of that.

It happened on the second night of his initiation, deep in the underground room with the other elder men telling the stories he needed to know, about the wars and great destruction that had plagued his ancestors and the problems that the people faced because of them. He had not eaten in days and there had been little sleep so he only half-heard it all and watched, instead, the fire in the center of the room where they sat. It was night; it was dark; it was quiet as the old men talked softly.

That's when he saw the fire come to life. The flickering flames gradually took form and shape; they became moving people, some running, and Kai leaned closer. He could almost make out individual faces against the background of chaos and collapse.

Then he heard the screams that broke the silence in great peals of agony and fear. He could feel this deeply, in his bones. The sounds rose and fell as he watched the people disappear under the molten debris from forms and structures of unfamiliar design and function. They melted in the intense heat as the people ran nowhere, making puny and pitiful attempts to shelter themselves with frail hands and arms. Kai watched as one woman placed her hand over her child's eyes in one last, futile effort of compassion before they, too, and a man near them sank under the ashes and the crush of bodies. Kai closed his own eyes, and jammed his hands over his ears to block out their screams.

When he looked up, the men were mysteriously gone;

only his uncle remained, and he was staring directly into Kai's wide, moist eyes, boring into his confusion like a spear shaft. "What you saw happened, a very long time ago. Those were our people; that is how they died. A terrible, painful end." The old man's eyes returned with familiar ease to the ashes of the slowly dying fire. "When I first saw this vision, I didn't know what it meant, either. It was too shocking, too painful, and the pain showed on my own face, as it shows on yours now. I cried. Like you, I was a boy who was trying to become a man but I broke down and cried in front of my own uncle on the night of my changing. I felt ashamed."

His face turned upward, as if to find an answer to the mystery of his shame in the darkness above him, or to hold back new tears by the sheer force of gravity. "At first, I thought I had failed, that they would send me back to my mother, still a boy. But they didn't. I became what I am, because I could look into the fire and have this image of our past. No one had done this before, and they made me what I am because I felt the pain, too. We are a feeling people. Our family, and our people, need leaders who know what it is to feel pain and suffering."

Slowly, his uncle rose. With great difficulty and pain, he struggled to his feet and gazed down at his young nephew wondering if he had actually been so young once and smooth as this boy. His memory would not confirm it, so it seemed impossible. Perhaps each generation got younger, more soft and unaware. "You have seen what only a few of us can see. You may become a leader yourself. Who knows? I see the potential in you now as you sit there wondering

21

what I am talking about and if you will be able to eat soon." So young. Where did that wonder and potential for astonishment go, and why did it go, when each day is like the last, one after another?

"Don't give up that wonder, but don't let it rule you either." He moved toward the ladder out of the room. Putting his right foot on the bottom rung, he paused for the strength to come and then looked over his shoulder for one, last time at Kai, the boy. "It begins tomorrow. The last steps. You can sleep now. But mostly you must remain quiet, to rest and regain your strength, and to remember every detail of the things you have seen and heard." He began the climb, then, to the wide ledge and the short, dark hallway leading to the door.

He stopped when the boy spoke. "Uncle, how do you know the vision in the fire is of the past?" The old man looked at him a long time from above before he responded. "Rest now, and don't question what you don't yet understand." He left.

The ways of his uncle's generation didn't make much sense. They took too long to do things that were for show and had little effect. And these things changed people. He and Shawn had been inseparable until Shawn's initiation. They had hunted, played at battle, built and rode their gliders high above the forests and valleys, until the older boy had become too large to stay aloft in the frail, delicate web of wood and fabric. Then, this too had ended, as all boyhood things dissolve in time. He stroked the thin blade upon the stone one last time.

All boyhood things had already ended for him, but he

was still a boy in the eyes of his people, still beyond the circle of men who spoke lofty words and determined how the future would look. A boy. Fit for boyhood chores but unfit to make serious decisions, and here he sat wanting with all his might to sink the thin blade into the throat of the man who took his sisters, the twins so young and happy. His hand twirled the knife, and his mother stirred in her sleep.

He looked back into the room. She appeared so frail and vulnerable in her sleep, and he thought ahead to his leave-taking. It would be hard for her, and for him. She would protest in front of the others, making him feel even more useless and immature, and he ached when he thought of seeing more grief in her eyes.

That's when it crept upon him, in this moment. The unthinkable, childish desire to run, and it became imbedded in his growing anger and resolve to get revenge, at all costs. But to use his knife, he had to get close to his target, and as he sat uselessly idle waiting for others to act, stroking the sharpening stone, his enemies put distance between them. Even if he could run without stopping, he could not overtake them before they reached the shelter of their mountains.

The mountains. Blue and distant, as seen from the crests of the low hills that rose gradually behind the village. He had never been close to them, and had been warned to stay far away from them since he learned to talk, but he had tempted fate by swooping close, but not too close, to them with Shawn on their gliders. Unfortunately, he did not know the trails there, except in the vagueness of stories about the last trips taken to them.

He stooped through the doorway and stood above his mother. Kneeling, he lightly brushed his lips against her forehead. It was warm and dry. He did the same to his brother, who tossed a bit from the contact, then settled back into his steady cycle of breathing.

From his corner, Kai took a carved, wooden play knife and placed it on the mat on which they slept. He wondered how his brother would react when he found it. Kai had carved it for a present.

He returned to the corner for a pale blue stone he kept hidden in an alcove in the wall above his bed. As he withdrew it, he went slightly dizzy, and his wounded shoulder gave a sharp twinge, but he straightened to walk back to his mother. He placed the rock in her open palm. This, too, made him dizzy and he thought of his long fast. He rose to pack more dried meat in his small pack. It would not do to run out.

Chapter Three
# Flight

For the first time in several days, he felt good and strong as his feet took him up the familiar path toward the top of the hill. He had been fortunate. He had encountered no one as he left the village, so his resolve had not been tested with questions from concerned friends or nosy adults. This made his plan seem even more plausible. He was moving, and that simple fact made a difference. His mind cleared as he climbed higher, and it tried to convince his stomach to be quiet. He hurried his steps so that his thoughts would not slow and dwell too long on what lay ahead. Physical action directed the mental.

The hills near the village were not high, but they were steep, so, spurred by his anxiety, he climbed fast, puffing as he fell into the opened space on top. His thighs and lungs burned from the climb. Once he had caught his breath, he rose and moved to the north end where a short, squat structure of rock and wood faced downward and into the forest. It was not used as a sentry post any longer. Now, the sentries walked the forest floor below the hill. He had never questioned why, but as he looked at the ruin, he recognized for the first time the spotted charring on the stones and knew how it had met its end. It was still, however, a place of mystery and seclusion that drew the young from the village. They came here to fight mock battles, playing at war and ruin, or, if they were older, to have the privacy necessary to learn of each other.

In Kai's case, it was used for storage. Along the back wall, partially hidden by strategically placed fallen beams and rocks, he found their gliders just as they had left them. His was on top, since he had used it a few times after Shawn became too heavy for his own. He set it aside, and drew out Shawn's. It was heavier, true, and clumsier, but he wondered if it might not be preferable to his own. He took it outside and began to assemble it on the grassy slope behind the hut, looking around him as he did.

The elders had ordered them to destroy the gliders and not to tell others how they were built. He and Shawn alone possessed that knowledge, now that the Crier was dead. The old recluse had taken a liking to the defiant boys and shown them how to build and use the gliders. Now he was gone from the disease before he could tell them why gliders were forbidden. It made no sense, but, then, many of the warnings he had been given seemed senseless, even stupid.

He had it only part way together when he found the first small hole in its wing. Something had eaten through the light fabric of fiber and resin, and then he found several more, increasingly larger, and two of the lashings that held the fabric to the frame were frayed and chewed. His heart sank.

Hurrying back to the hut, he pulled his own glider onto the hillside. His fingers twitched slightly as he hurried to lay the frame out flat on the grass, and then, in his haste, he almost punctured one wing on a sharp rock as he unfolded its light fabric.

He stopped. He knelt down, looking off to the north and the tops of the trees, green and calmly waving in the slight breeze that, even as he knelt, began to dry the beads of sweat on his forehead. The short grass under him was light colored and dry. He could hear something small and shy moving in the brush behind him but did not care to investigate.

The trees were unconcerned with this one small boy, or his lost sisters. He felt comforted by the thought, and took a deep breath, only to let it out slowly, and then take another. He needed to work quickly, but he also needed to control himself, and to do things correctly or he would make his job even more difficult, and perhaps deadly.

Calmed, he returned to the hut and retrieved his bag, bow and arrows, laying them on the grass near his glider. He finished unfolding it, and was lightened when he found the wings intact, the frame sturdy yet still flexible. There would be no need to repair it. He sat down and took a chunk of dried meat from his pack, chewing it well, savoring the rich juices that slowly brought his stomach back to life. It began to rumble loudly, and then glow as he finished, swallowing just enough of the jerky to keep his insides occupied, yet not enough to make them cramp. He took only a half mouthful of water, not wanting to dilute the strength of the meat. His throat and stomach both hurt as he swallowed. The days of fasting before the attack had taken a toll.

Now, it was a simple matter, and in a few moments he had the frame lashed together and the crossbar in position.

He tied the harness that would hold him under the wide wings into place, then the stirrups that tied in two places along the lower main frame, and the central support to which the wings attached. It was frail, indeed, as he hoisted it for a test, to recollect its heft and points of balance. The blue haze of the mountains in the distance appeared even more remote than usual as he felt the weight of the craft and remembered how tiring the cramped harness and stirrups were.

He sat back on the grass and took another, long look at the forest, hill and sky. Before he shouldered his pack, he walked to the rear wall of the hut and peed on the grass. He did not know when, or where for that matter, he would touch the ground again, and that thought was unnerving. This was not like the flights he and Shawn enjoyed.

With his pack and weapons firmly tied behind him, he slipped into the harness. The wind had died down, but the day was warm and he knew the breeze would stiffen in the mid-day heat that would force strong updrafts from the forest and meadows. Almost as if calling him to action, the tall dried grass stirred at his feet. He leaped down the slope taking long, loping strides, then sprang for the air; for a moment he felt the light elation of being airborne, which ended when he felt the weight of gravity take hold bringing him back down with a dull shocking thud a short ways downhill. He almost tumbled, but was able to slide with the rough gravel and loose soil and balance the glider away from harm at the same time. He began the steep trudge back to the top, complicated by the weight and awkward expanse of the glider.

It took three tries, but on the fourth he finally found his chest and arms straining against the harness as he and the glider floated on the warm air. He fumbled his feet into the dangling loops of the stirrups and tried to get comfortable in the cramped, curled position while simultaneously trying to concentrate on the vagaries of the wind, the direction of the mountains.

The breeze, however, was not quite right. When he tried to force his way toward the north, he lost altitude quickly, so he was forced to make a turn to the right and to use the hill's updraft to spiral higher in search of the stronger, the prevalent winds. In this way he would be able to tack toward the mountains, but it also meant that he would have to go once over the village. Bracing into the turn, he hoped that people were still inside, waiting, withdrawn, in shock. He did not want someone to sound the alarm before he was too far to be recalled.

Shifting his weight and applying more pressure with his right foot, Kai was able to bank the craft in closer to the hill. He had not thought of his shadow until it was almost too late, but by holding dangerously close to the hill it fell on brush and trees rather than houses and paths. He was learning.

As he looked down, the village appeared to have recaptured much of its former tranquility. From this distance, from this perspective, it seemed placid and ordered, except for the three, blackened ruined buildings that marred the panorama. Few people stirred, and those who were outside were walking toward the Shelter looking down to the ground, their backs to the hill, completely oblivious to the scene above them.

He appeared a graceful bird in its swoop on the wind, slightly banking around the curve of the hill yet intent upon the scene below. He was a hawk, a falcon, a bird of prey and as the village disappeared behind him, he turned his gaze to what was ahead. The wind began to roar across his body, rippling the taut wings and the rigid frame. Its lashings creaked. He felt his hope rise with the wind, and he tightened his grip on the crossbar and looked to the mountains.

At the best of times it was no easy task to make the glider do what he wanted it to do. Wasted as he was by lack of food and sleep, Kai began to feel the terrifying enormity of his plan. When it unfolded in his imagination, it did so like all his inspirations, quickly and passionately, carrying its own blind persuasion.

Sitting in front of his home, there had been only a brief image of him springing into the air with his glider, at first as a means of escaping the frustrating inactivity of his people, but the word escape took hold and he thought of the attackers again and one thing connected to another until he had a clear image of him dropping on his horror-struck and faceless enemy to have his revenge as his sisters watched in admiration and gratefulness.

Now, as he gazed off into the distance, and as he was forced time and time again to take a zigzag course away from and seemingly never toward the mountains he desired, he realized just how difficult it would be, and how long it might take. More importantly he began, not to doubt, but to question that brief image of revenge, and the decision that came so quickly from it.

He would need to stop several times to rest, and that meant sleep, and this also meant finding places to land, places from which he could find the wind to get up in the air again. And in this moment of questioning and concern about his mission, the voice spoke to him for the first time since that night in the Shelter, the night of his initiation, the night of the attack.

It was not exactly a voice, but more of a sudden intense feeling that demanded attention. It had been with him as long as he could remember, perhaps even before he learned to talk with his mother, and it had gotten him out of scrapes, but more often into trouble. When it came, he would talk with it in the normal, everyday voice inside his head. It seldom answered. Sometimes, he would try to reason with it, trying to avoid what he knew would be wrong—no, not wrong, maybe not wise would be more accurate—but more often than not losing the argument.

For the last few days, events had kept it quiet. There had been the need to do as the old men told him, and then his attempt to understand his dream and the horror he saw in the fire. All of this was forgotten as he followed the flow of events from the attack. Even as he made his plan, the voice didn't chime in to offer advice, but he hadn't noticed its absence. Now, however, it was here, strong and insistent. It was firm and demanding and it was telling him to land. He shut it off with a song about the forests and focused on his flying.

However, once more it proved right. He stayed too long

in the harness the first time, pushing his strength and endurance to the limits. The pain grew too strong to be avoided so he finally allowed his body to have its say and began searching for a suitable landing spot. He took the first that came along: a small mound off the overgrown trail he was trying to follow toward the mountains. By the time he had circled the hill twice, he had chosen an open space and began his approach.

What Kai had not considered were his cramped muscles and their reluctance to respond. His approach went well. He had used his arms and weight all along to maneuver the glider to the spot he had chosen. But when he made the sudden shift to try to point his glider up the slope for an easy, gradual landing, he found his legs would not move. The landing was flawless, except for one thing. One leg remained in its stirrup. Off balance, he fell headlong into the rocks and short grass of the hillside. The crossbar snapped in two and he buried his face into the gritty soil. He lay there until the sound of the wind in the grass and the treetops below came back to him.

Untangling himself from the harness proved difficult because he didn't want to put any stress on the wing frames. After several anxious heartbeats while he flexed his hands, he felt the tingle of circulation returning to his fingertips and began to work on the reluctant knots. Crawling out from under the glider, he stood erect. His muscles screamed, and he dropped to the ground to let them unravel slowly. He rubbed them; he talked to them, slowly kneading the circulation and therefore the life back into his extremities. Again he stood, this time wobbly, but straight.

He turned his attention to the glider. Except for the crossbar, it remained undamaged, so he undid his pack and removed two pieces of meat to eat as he looked for a replacement. He had gone only a short distance when he was hit by the oddest, unfamiliar sensation. His backbone tingled, and perspiration began to trickle from his armpits down his ribs. He undid the thongs that held his soft, leather shirt, but he was not warm, really. It was a cold, chilling feeling. The suddenness of its arrival stopped him in his tracks. He thought of the voice, but then the dream. He had felt like this in the dream as he looked out over the huge expanse of grasslands.

He looked around him. There appeared to be no danger, but he returned to the glider and carried it a short distance to some low brush. He covered it as best he could without further risking damage to it, and he hid his pack in another bush nearby. Taking his bow, he moved cautiously, working his way along the slope of the hill, through its narrow band of brush and stunted trees. The feeling would not leave him, but he put it aside and focused upon his search.

He could not find a branch long enough and straight enough for the crossbar. On the hill, they were gnarled and twisted into odd shapes, so he worked his way downward, toward the base and the taller trees that surrounded the mound. It felt good to be moving again, active after so long a ride. To be hunting, in a way, as he chose his way downward with care and greater deliberation. Thus, a person moves well, he had been taught. After a momentary pause, he stepped into the fringe of the forest where it was dark, cool, refreshing.

He had not traveled very far when he caught the slim scent of something almost familiar. Something vague, like a memory that pops up foggy and undefined. It was not a common smell, but not unknown either. Soft, sweet, like a spice but not one from the forest. He slowed, and began to move into the breeze. The scent grew more distinct, although it was only periodically present, coming in brief wisps. He suddenly struck a trail and, without thinking, he stepped abruptly back into the shelter of a tree. From there, he could survey the path, the exposed dirt, the grasses.

Slowly, he panned his surroundings, looking for movement and fearing he might find it too late. He knelt for a close look at the trail. There had been several feet across it, and recently, and they traveled together. He saw isolated, individual tracks that stood out from the confusion of the others, and was taken by their odd character. They were not rounded, contoured, with the blurred outlines of footwear, as human feet and their tracks should be. They were flat and uniform, with sharp outlines and two abrupt levels. Although he had not realized it at the time, he had seen these signs before, as he climbed from the broken ruin of the Shelter, and once again as he sat outside his home preparing for this journey, staring at nothing but recording anyway the identical repetitive imprints in the dirt before him near the door to his home. He had been blind. These were the tracks of the raiders.

His first reaction brought with it an unsettling confusion. What type of being was he chasing? From the old stories his uncle and the Crier told, he had concluded that they were like him, but there were also the odd, almost contradictory reports that they were hideous creatures: cold-blooded, unfeeling and calculating. He had taken these as exaggerations meant to frighten unruly children, but now, he did not know. Perhaps these things were not human after all. Perhaps they were, but different, with unusual forms. He did not know. He felt fear edge in closer to him.

There was one other thing that troubled him even more, and it brought back the chilled sensation he felt on the hill. These tracks should not be here. He was far from the trail the raiders took from the village. He had followed that one all day, cutting across its almost obscured course time and time again as it wove its way in the most direct route to the mountains. He could see it from the air at times, a slight suggestion or indentation in the patterns of treetops, a worn place in meadows. Although ancient, it was kept fresh by animals and erosion. He had not lost its course, but now, here, far to the west, another trail with signs of the raiders.

Why had they moved to this other trail? Doing it cost them time. Would they be so frightened by his people's pursuit that they would try to evade them? No. The marks were open and apparent; they had not taken the pains to hide their route. Were they so certain that his people would be so slow to follow? Another nagging thought kept surfacing, and Kai did not like it. Had there been two raiding parties, or had one party split into two groups for protection? One to act as a rear guard while the other escaped? He did not know.

So, he followed the trail, at first walking on its path, slowing as it curved around a tree, then a large rock where a raider could be waiting in hiding. To be safe, he stepped into the trees and paralleled its course, but this was too slow and difficult. When he decided to step back into the trail and take his chances, he caught once again the scent, and this time it was strong and close. He froze.

There was an opening ahead. He could barely trace its outline through the trees, its lighter quality showing where it began. He circled to his right, keeping low and flitting silently from late afternoon shadow to shadow. They seemed to deepen even as he moved between them. He came to the meadow from its east side, far from the point at which the trail entered it. From a fringe of low bushes, he could see it whole, yet remain unseen.

At first, the discomfort of lying full upon the bunched grasses and sticks from generations of bushes did not bother him. His concentration was elsewhere. However, slowly these small bodily pains seeped into his consciousness. Nothing moved, nothing happened, and no one appeared to be in ambush, so he moved to his left and smoothed out a place for his body in the sandy soil. Bending two branches of the bush in front of him down, slowly, he was able once more to focus on the whole clearing.

On the farthest side in a small alcove against the fringe of the forest, he saw the charred remains of a fire. The scent he had followed had had a tinge of smoke to it, but also an odd, uncommon flavor mixed in it.

He slowly dropped back into the trees behind him and circled around the edge of the clearing, being careful to strike the trail well beyond the point where it exited the clearing. He crossed it and continued on his circuit, noting the tracks that marked the raiders' course on the sandy path. They were too overlapped, too jumbled and, oddly, too uniform in size and shape to differentiate. He did not take time to stop and try to count the number of the individuals who made them. Intent on his goal, he moved quickly around the meadow to the brush line of the alcove near the fire. Nothing moved. The breeze provided the only sound as it made its way through the silent trees. He took a deep breath from it as it stroked his sweaty skin, and with his bow drawn and arrow nocked, he stepped into the dim afternoon daylight.

Nothing happened. Nothing moved. He surveyed the brush line along the whole meadow, and then moved closer to the fire. There were several indentations in the grass around it. From their lengths and their effects upon the grasses, he decided the raiders had rested a long time in this one spot, but for how long? How sure were they that they were not being pursued? He looked back up the trail, wondering if they would leave men to wait. He felt the ashes. They were cold.

He counted the beds: ten. But had they posted guards as the others took their rest? Had they changed guards? He made a circle wide of the fire. Ten beds, but one that was wider than the others, perhaps a bit shorter. He once more scanned the circling brush line, and then moved closer to the unique bed.

His heart stopped. He bent to it and it almost seemed as if he could feel the body heat still clinging to the soil. He put his face close to the ground and could easily convince himself that his sisters' smell lingered, their presence persisted. He rose and circled the bed. In the sparse grass near it he found a single, unmistakable footprint. A human foot had made it, a small one. He raised his gaze and looked northward. He had found his sisters, alive. At least, they were alive when the fire was alive.

His people, when they finally finished their endless chatting and acted, would follow the wrong trail. If they found tracks on the main trail, they would stay to it while his sisters were dragged along this old, abandoned track.

He returned to the charred circle. No pit had been dug. They had just heaped up large pieces of wood and set them ablaze, so someone had been the fire carrier. Maybe seven fighters, with perhaps one or two to carry fire and tend to their prisoners. Much of the wood was green and remained unburned. They had stupidly torn branches from living trees, a few from those that had fallen. It had been a sick fire. Why had he not seen the smoke? More importantly, why would they make smoke if they were trying to confuse the search party? As always, more questions than answers but the voice in him was firm. The raiders had an intricate plan and he needed to be smart, and he must be patient.

But then the odd smell returned; he placed his face above the coals. It was there. It coated the back of his tongue as he drew it in. Then the night of the attack came back to him, the air heavy with the smells of destruction, the collapse of the building around him. His arms ached with the exertion of digging his way out, and his eyes began to water. The smell took on the character of all things evil. And the raiders carried that smell.

Withdrawing into the cover of the trees again, he cut a wide arc and caught the trail well away from the clearing and any traps. On its open surface, he began to trot back the way he had come. The logs in the fire were still smoldering when he had rolled them over, and live, hot coals gleamed in the ashes. They had spent the remainder of the night here and left in the morning. He had narrowed the gap. And with this thought came the uncomfortable elation of knowing that his plan was working.

The new crossbar was green, so it flexed when he put weight upon it. This unusual springiness made it difficult for him to get airborne again, but after three tries on the short hill he was fortunate enough to find a vagrant updraft, and then, making adjustments for the repair, he coaxed his light craft up over the trees.

It was late and in the gathering twilight he knew he could not go far before being forced to find a place for the night. But he was too close to stop now. The discovery of the trail, and the beds, spurred him to push on, to defy the limits of his physical endurance, and the darkness itself. Feeling closer than he had hoped to be after so little time had elapsed since his last talk with Luther, he knew that he must close the gap some more before he could rest.

However, as the evening wind tossed him about, forcing him to lean, flex and compensate, and as the shadows below lengthened and began to wrap the forest below in their darkness, he began to lose the path. His impulse dulled. Tired, drowsy yet alert, he rationalized his way toward the ground. There would be time and, he understood then, without rationalization but through instinct, perhaps, or the intuition of the voice at least, that he should not overtake them before he had rested and eaten. He would have to think up a plan that would allow one young man to defeat nine or ten grown men.

The number of mounds below him had increased since he last stopped as he neared the mountain range of the north, and they were bigger. This gratefully made his choice easier, so selecting the tallest in a group of three near him, he began his spiral downward toward it, keeping his eyes alert for openings large enough for a landing. He had not completed the first circuit, however, when he caught the first whiff of that curious scent. It was strong and persistent, and in the next instant he saw thin wisps of smoke rising from the trees and brush at the mound's base, disappearing into the twilight.

He banked sharply away from the hill, almost too sharply. He fell away as he lost the breeze and for a brief, giddy heartbeat felt himself on the verge of plunging into the trees below. But he corrected, and with the help of the green flexibility of the new crossbar caught air again to slip around the curve of the next nearest hill in the group. A figure eight would bring him to it, but there was no time to be picky about finding a place to land. To do so would leave him exposed too long, and although relatively silent in his passing, the quiet evening forest would not cover the rippling of his wings.

He cut the figure eight short and banked sharply out over the forest to complete a loop for a direct uphill approach against the wind. Again, he turned too sharply and as he twisted and leaned trying to keep what little air he had to lift his wings, he shook his feet loose from the stirrups. Although he needed to be free as soon as he touched ground, this maneuver complicated matters, for he began to drop too quickly. But the wind gusted against his face, so the cumulative effects of dropping and the increased speed from the turn provided the forward momentum necessary. Scraping the top of one tree with his left knee, he raised the other leg to miss the last tree before he dropped into a small, rocky clearing, if not perfectly, at least safely. His bowman's eye had saved him.

He undid the harness and rolled out from under the wings. Anxious, but fully alert and in control again, he quickly scanned the glider where it lay. The greenness of the crossbar had saved it this time, but the lashings on one wing were loosened and his knees and right elbow were scraped and full of cinders. These would heal. The lashings, however, were another matter. They were old and brittle, and to try to re-lash them would be futile. He needed new ones, but he had no material or time to make them. But, the voice came again and he knew that he may not need the glider again if the raiders are bedded down for the night.

He retied as best he could with the sash from his food bag, and then carried the glider into the surrounding brush. There, he laid it gently on the tops of some short bushes and cut branches to cover it part way. It would be impossible to see, except from very close by, or from the air. He sat under it for a moment, and ate some more of the meat as he waited for the day to end. After a long drink from his rawhide bag, he took another, long, silent moment to ask the powers of his world to help him and his sisters. Going to the edge of the downslope of the hill, he moved slowly around it until he could see the slight column of smoke from the fire in the growing darkness.

~

By the time Kai covered the distance between hills and climbed silently partway up the one above their camp, it was late. The fire was full and bright in the distance at first, but as he crept closer it died down, lighting only the lower branches of the closest trees. He came in from above them and through the tangle of undergrowth that separated the tree trunks. It took time to avoid the unseen obstacles as he felt his way by reading the slant and sweep of bushes and contours of trees as if he were reading the wrinkles on his mother's face. He had time now. They would not move until morning, but he needed to move wisely. His training took over without effort or conscious relinquishment. His mind wormed its way through the problems and complications before him, and he moved well, so his disappointment was great when he pushed aside the last limb, to find the campsite deserted.

In the dying firelight he could make out the bent grasses, the places where tree branches had been wrenched away from the trunks and one whole sapling felled to provide the crude, smoky fire.

And that is when Kai suddenly understood its purpose and the voice in his head shouted out their plan. He felt the fear hovering over him, waiting to drop like a rock. He slowly let the branch rise back into its old place, but he was not quick enough. It came off in his hand as the air in front of him burst into bright light with a roar. The hair and skin below his upraised arm was seared by the blast.

The pain did not have time to register. His mind was too suddenly committed to the one thing. Survival. He rolled to his right and into the cover of tangled brush. He had to move quietly and quickly away from the fire and into the darkness and open terrain, undetected. There he could use his bow. Here, it was useless, an encumbrance. Although the curvature of the bow fit that of his back and haunches, he could feel the quiver touch something and then snag as he made his way lizard-like through stunted bushes.

There was another flash and roar, behind and to his left. He could smell its terrible effect on the plants. It was the same scent that had haunted him for the last day, from the night in the village and to the campsite in the meadow: the sweet stench of living matter suddenly changed to fire and cinder. He paused. Had his enemy misjudged his position and direction, or had he simply lighted another torch, the better to see Kai?

Around him, the forest listened, completely silent except for the crackle of the burning branches. Taking a deep, shaky breath, he exhaled slowly as he placed one hand before the other, one knee pushing him forward, and then the other. He paused again. This time when he drew in his breath and held it, he felt the presence and then heard a slight rustle of the brush off to his left. His breath came easier, and as he exhaled, he scanned the immediate area. There were only two trees close, one to the left and ahead, one slightly behind to his right. He heard it again, near the same place, and from then on, it was repeated, with slight variations but also regularity.

Kai quickly considered his dilemma, trying to slow his heart by regulating his breathing. It's beating too loudly; he'll hear it, he must hear it. But then the question came:

how many? If there were two, or more, he was dead. One thing at a time, the voice swelled up inside him.

To confront the one coming from his left, he must step behind the tree to his right. This would expose him to any others hiding nearby. If he went to his left, he would be exposed to the man approaching. If he backed to his right, the tree on the left, if he waited long enough, would afford him the half-heart beat it would take to stand and step behind the trunk. Half a beat of exposure to anyone else waiting for him to make a fatal mistake.

The one approaching decided it. This was reality, a certainty, the reality that would not slow to allow him to weigh all his options. He waited a few beats as the other covered a bit more of the distance, then rose stiffly, unintentionally tensing in anticipation of the flash, and stepped behind the tree. Relieved, he stooped to draw the bow over his shoulder and straightened to his full height. He nocked an arrow and waited, leaning into the rough bark of the trunk scraping his back.

For a short time there was no more sound. They both waited. Then, the other moved off, putting distance between them. The light from the bush was dying, so Kai suddenly decided to use the raider's own device. He stooped to the ground and, keeping his eyes on the darkness ahead, groped for a stone, a stick, anything heavy, his fingers closing instinctively around a fist-sized rock. He stood again and threw it wide, to the opposite side of the burning bush. If the old ruse worked and the enemy moved in that direction, he would have time for one, perhaps two shots as he crossed the opening between them using the fire to blind the raider.

One shot here, and one as he, himself, covered the distance to the other tree for another angle, and to nock another arrow behind its protection. He drew the string taut.

He heard the raider move closer. At first Kai could hear the leaves and smaller limbs brush his shoulders and thighs with an odd, unnatural scraping sound. But then he more than heard as his senses extended beyond and outward and the feeling of the voice came back like a cold, soft hand stroking his backbone, fingers massaging the temples of his aching head. Inexplicably, he began to relax. He did not become less intent, or less afraid, only more relaxed and resigned to what must come. His enemy was almost out of the shadows and into the light of the fire. He could feel him there, almost see with his mind's eye as he worked his way to where the heavy stone had fallen. He was confident, a hunter like Kai, sure of himself.

Kai slowly peered around the curve of the trunk, not to verify, only to prepare for his shot, keeping his taut bow lowered, his back straight, now, and rolling lightly off the rough, cold tree bark. A shape began to form at the edge of the darkness. It froze. The trap was sensed. Kai did not hesitate. Stepping clear of the tree he let his arrow go, all in one smooth motion that did not end but propelled him forward after its release and into the lee of the other, the closer tree. His second arrow was out by then and nocked, beats before the flash came splintering the bark at the height of his head on the tree he had just left. Flames and horrid smoke rose instantaneously with a muffled groan, perhaps a curse, as he stepped free of his shelter to face, finally, his enemy.

The raider had tripped as he dodged the first arrow. Kai realized this almost too late, but in the blinding instant he cleared the tree into full view he did not realize or think, only reacted and felt almost surprise at the release of the second arrow toward the man, bent over and trying to regain his balance, no sign of a weapon or threat. Kai froze, watching the flight of the arrow with a debilitating curiosity that was not hate nor fear nor morbidity, only wonder and consuming interest. He had no thought of stepping back into the shelter of his tree, or running. He simply waited between the abnormally slow beats of his heart.

The arrow took him in the small triangle of the left collarbone. There was a small rift in his garment there, although Kai had not perceived it until the protruding shaft drew his attention to it, and to the well of blood that had been tapped. It spurted out and stained the raider's shirt from the point at which the arrow entered, down the front. So much blood. So quickly.

The raider tried to stand erect, and in the brief span of time between the effort and the fall, Kai perceived two things. First, the clothing. With the exception of the eyes, the raider was completely covered—hair, nose, mouth, legs—with the exception of the place where the arrow had entered, the small opening that Kai now realized was the place where a hood draped over his shirt. It was terrifying, this impression created by the darkness of the clothing, a bleak, almost black, grayness with only the two eyes distinct against its background. And the eyes were the other thing that caught him. They were sad, hollow affairs, and there were dark circles below them. In shape and dimension, they were human-like, almost familiar, as was the raider's overall body form. But Kai could not be certain in that brief instant as it fell.

He knew what must be done. He must make certain and at least disarm his enemy, but he balked again. He withdrew behind the tree and leaned against its cold, uncomfortable certitude. His heart raced; his mind floundered, as if all his bodily and mental functions had been forestalled until this moment, and now must make up the time lost. He squatted on his haunches, closer to the ground, as his hands began to shake uncontrollably. His breathing came in short gasps as his whole frame quaked. His mind raced, fighting for the control he felt quickly ebbing away. He held his breath, searching the darkness for danger, diversion. There was only the sound of his wounded foe, now hidden by the brush, its breathing raspy and sporadic.

The bow slid from his hand against his will, and Kai wept. The possibility of the moment had dogged his life, as it did for all his people, and yet it had been merely a remote possibility. A possibility that one day he would try to kill another. They had played at it. He had learned his skills in games, by slaying imaginary beings, distant, vague and threatening, a friend who crumbled and collapsed only to rise up again an instant later laughing and taunting.

Now this. This being was not rising. This being was not taunting. Instead, its breathing became even more irregular and labored, and it drew Kai's full concentration to it. The shaking slowly ceased as he looked off into the night sky and listened. His ears ached with the intensity of their work. The darkness descended around them. The silence intensified. He wanted to walk away, find his glider and go home.

He knew what he must do, and that knowledge raised a primal dread, of death and sickness and pain, and the confusion of desires for the foe's quick death and fear that it might not live. He prayed that what was in those strange clothes was not human. A monster from the stories would be easier to kill. Then, he had no heart to kill even a monster and pleaded with the night that this being live, that the weapon had been dropped far beyond its reach and that it could not move to it, that Kai could approach, or leave, unharmed. But his fear grew. To go there meant certain exposure. Perhaps sudden and painful death, from the dying foe, or another of the raiders.

His gaze had descended to the ground. He looked above him again. In the dark, he could discern the points of light, steady and unconcerned with the life of one small boy, perhaps with a whole people. This expansiveness, this vastness consoled him. The voice settled it, with a simple urge to go.

Well, what are you going to do? The sound of his own, whispered voice surprised him. He had not heard a spoken voice for what seemed to be a long, long time. It consoled him, as well, clarifying things in a way. Using the tree for support, he slowly pushed himself upward. The bow was at his feet. He looked down to it. If I die, I will die well, he thought. And if he could save his foe, he would. He would approach without threat. He took a very deep breath, and he thought of his family.

The whine was high in pitch and inhuman. It was horrifying and it increased in volume at an alarming rate. Kai dropped back into a crouch behind the tree, his hands going automatically first to his bow, but then to his ears. The volume increased beyond bounds, each increase an expansion of the pain. It was deafening, even with his hands pressing with all his might against his skull. He could feel its intensity throughout his whole body. When it seemed he could not take any more, there was a dull concussion and a sharp, brilliant flash. Even in the lee of the tree, sheltered from the direct, intense heat of the blast, Kai was singed instantly. The exposed grasses near his feet wilted into crisp shafts that were consumed without ever bursting into flame.

He took his hands down. The whine had died suddenly away leaving behind an incredible, ringing absence broken only by the crackling of the fire burning the brush and trees around him. He cautiously peered around the trunk. Where his foe had fallen there was a hole in which rocks were charred and melted together, and from which smoke rose skyward. Smoke, and that smell. The brush burned, and the trees within a roughly oblong area were smoldering, their bark now charcoal. There was no sign of the raider, only the dense and repugnant odor of dissolved matter.

Kai fell to his knees behind the tree and vomited. He had little in his stomach, so he retched and convulsed until he fell headlong, exhausted, to the ground, sobbing inconsolably. The eyes were there, in the dark night into which he plunged. They were watching him.

Chapter Four
# Killer

He awoke under his glider. At first, he had no recollection of where he was. The ground, hard and uneven, made his back ache from sleeping too long in one position. He groaned as he tried to roll over onto his right side, so he stopped and took the time to survey his surroundings and allow his memory to wake. It did not take long. As his body began to come to life, his memory came back in a rush like the intense, awful dread of a very recent, a very bad dream.

He sat up. His stomach churned within him, and he was not sure if it was hunger that made it protest, or revulsion at the troubling memories of the night and the images that swept in without warning. He had had to stop several times to become ill on the return trip from the raider trap, and even now that trip was alive with all the sensual details—the smells, the feelings, the taste of charred matter on the back of his tongue—that would not leave despite the repeated attempts to spew it from him.

Fortunately, before the memory of those senses could capture his whole being, the reality of the moment intruded. His armpit began to sting from the wound. The night before, he had not felt it fully until he began the walk

51

back to the glider, and then, when the pain became too intense to bear, he matted some leaves and dirt, turned to mud with the little saliva he was able to coax forth, and applied them to the wound. It was a haphazard affair, and most of the tiny compress had fallen off before he reached his camp, but he had been too tired and disoriented to care. Now, the burned slash was swollen, with hot, red edges. It was narrow in width, but it extended down a portion of his inner biceps and moved in a broken line down to his upper ribs. It was not deep, but sensitive where the skin lay open and exposed to the air. He wished he knew only half the medicines of old Crier, but he was inexperienced, and his education in these types of things was to have begun after his initiation. Now, he missed it dreadfully.

He touched the wound gingerly. It smarted. He poured a little water over it, thinking as he did that he would have to find more somewhere, and soon. The coolness helped for the moment. Now, partially clean and seen in the light of day, it did not seem so large, so bad. The arm was the worst, but the heat had cauterized the flesh in places, so he hoped it would heal quickly and of its own accord. He looked upward to the light of day, wondering if he would be able to maneuver the glider.

He looked off toward the mountains. He had never been this close, even in the air. It was such a short distance, actually, but it was a new and foreign land to him. The trees and the plant life were much the same as his home, but there was little sign of game. Birds were singing to the dawn, but only a few, and this compounded his sense of solitude, deepening his awareness of his own vulnerability and with this came paranoia, a growing instinct or feeling that he was being watched, led, manipulated.

When he was younger, these feelings of powerlessness resulted not in resignation, but in defiance and a firm commitment to evade his watchers and ruin their plans of control. It was so today, as well. He would get his sisters back, but whether or not he would make their captors pay had become a point of troublesome contention. His anger and determination were still strong, but his will to cause pain was silent.

He turned to the glider and began to gather his things together. He did not take time to sit and eat, but just took two short drinks of water and then two pieces of meat to chew as he worked.

The morning was cool and refreshing, but its beauty was dulled by the experiences of the night before and the realization that the wind was a mere hint and the hill smaller than he had thought when he chose it as a landing spot in the twilight. As he worked at the lashings he kept checking, hoping the wind would increase, but by the time he had tied the strips of bark and rawhide scavenged from his bag and clothes into place, there was still too little wind for his needs. He would not return to the taller hill by the raiders' camp and the third hill in the group was smaller than this one. He decided to fold the glider and look for a better place along the trail northward. The day had warmed and as he shouldered his load he was glad he would not have to fly right away because his arm was stiffening and when he extended it, it stung.

Despite this, he felt good, moving through the cool dawn

forest, away from the hill with its blackened hole, away from thoughts of it as his motions concentrated his mind on the immediate and necessary and physical.

After the drugged rest from fatigue, he moved quickly but cautiously. The trail climbed gradually but consistently, and curved around the increasingly steep foothills. It had many switchbacks that required him to slow down and feel his way step by step, anticipating, with each, another searing blast. And then the trail would open and his body would slip back into the easy rhythms of the soft lope and swing of his load. His eyes developed their own pattern, scanning the trail ahead and the cover along its sides, and then dipping down to the path itself and the dirt and grass immediately in front of him.

The tracks were fresh, from the evening before of course, and now that he had the time to study them over a long distance for an extended period of time, he began to sense their own rhythm as well. They were not rushed. Instead, each was evenly spaced for a simple walk, no extended reaches, no deepened heel prints, or toe, with dust flung backwards into little piles. They were in no hurry, and even the footprints of his sisters, when they were apparent within the crush of the others, seemed to be paced at an easy walk. Were they so certain that pursuit would take so long? Or that their one, lone sentry would so easily turn back any hotheads, like Kai?

Before the morning had passed, he found the hill he needed, one set off from the slope of the foothills, steep and opened on the top. The breeze had stiffened as well up against the shoulder of the foothills, so his confidence rose with it when he found a stream falling down the hill's slope.

It was near the pool at the base that he found the second camp, nearly identical to the first. The fire, the indentations of the beds in the open, all was as it was before. The twins had slept last night in the sand together, their contours and prints easily discernible. The fire was still smoldering, and warm, so he was close behind them.

Ignoring the tingling along his spine that wanted him to rush on, he took the time to bathe in the pool and soak his wound as the early afternoon warmed. They would be moving slower up the slope. He could catch up easily. His resolve was intact, but he no longer relished the idea of a confrontation. In fact, the possibility began to sicken him, but before it could catch hold, he ducked under the water into the cool depths and washed himself clean. Then he sat on the rocks to dry, his bow, with one arrow nocked, next to him while the quiver leaned against the rock.

It was in this moment of relative calm that the full enormity of what was to come settled down upon him like a ruin. It chilled and oppressed. He had no real plan. He had only vague hopes. His goal was simple: to free his sisters. Failing this, he would slow the raiders' escape until his people could catch up. Both seemed reasonable, both possible. But he didn't know how he might accomplish either.

He was operating at a great disadvantage. He didn't know the land. And I am alone, he thought, alone. One boy, not even a man really. There were at least seven raiders with deadly weapons ahead. There would be more in their village. He looked up to the sky. The voice was silent, as if waiting.

Luther said that one aspect of wisdom was to see strength

in weakness, weakness in strength. Kai had not known what that meant and considered it just another of the odd riddles adults spoke to make themselves appear wiser and more experienced than the young people to whom they spoke. Now, however, he had an inkling of what the old man was getting at with his cryptic words.

His weakness, at this one moment in time, must be turned into strength, if not by luck then by sheer force of will. He was small and alone and they would not be expecting one lone person. He could move easily and perhaps avoid detection. Unlike a large party, he could run, and hide. The raiders were clumsy in their numbers, hopefully even arrogant in their superiority. He would use that if he could.

Rising from the rock, he still did not have a plan, but he had an emerging, faint trust in his own ability to use circumstance to his benefit. And he was patient, now that he was so close. He would wait; he would see; he would act when the opportunity came. Again, one feeling pulsed inside his head, and if he could put it into a word, it would be "yes."

Dressing in the warm light, he began to regret his bath. It had cleaned the wound well enough, but now it was soft and pliant, and it hurt when his arm stretched. Steeling himself, he pulled his shirt on over his head. He would not let this wound slow him. If he moved normally, it would heal normally. Shouldering his load, he started up the hill. It was steep, but he was refreshed and eager to be done.

The mid-day warmth had brought with it the usual, stiff wind. On the first try, he was in the air again, trying to hang to one side to favor his wounded arm. To complicate matters, the trail was more difficult to follow in the maze of trees and ravines below; the openings were fewer as the forest rose densely up the flanks of the mountain.

If the old stories were accurate, they once had waited for Kai's people on these slopes. Once his people had even penetrated farther—almost to the clear, rocky slopes above the trees. Beyond this, only mystery. Each time many of his people had died from ambushes, but they went back time and time again, trying each possible route up the incline only to be slaughtered from above. It had been hopeless, futile, insane, but noble.

And this gave him the seed of a plan. He would adopt the raiders' own strategy. He would land ahead, uphill of them, and wait for them to come to him on his own terms. To do so, however, he must know which ravine their trail followed. The wind had taken him away from it several moments before, and he dreaded the necessity to cut back and forth, perhaps several times, to rediscover its path. He was an exposed target waiting for one up-cast set of eyes to betray him. So he decided to use the strong wind in his favor by making one quick, direct tack up the mountain. Once above the tree line, he could zigzag the meadows where three primary canyons sloped down toward his village. The trail had to emerge from one, so he could land, reconnoiter, and watch from hiding. The slope had steepened so they could not have moved very quickly. They would need one more night before reaching the summit. He had time, and he would use it well.

It was a short, swift trip up the mountain, but finding a landing spot was more difficult than he had imagined. Once the tall trees were left behind, there were ample open places among the wind-blown and stunted growth, but each time he tried an approach he was buffeted by the undeflected crosswinds from the deep ravines that wanted to drive him farther along, over a cliff or into rocks. The winds were not only strong, but confusing, rising as they did up the three different canyons only to meet and battle for dominance.

Finally, tired and therefore acting too hastily, he decided to risk dropping down to tree-top level and making one up-hill approach, hoping to touch just where one steep ridge peaked and the conflicting wind from its other side would slow him at the peak.

It could have worked, and in the final instant it appeared as if it might, but the winds were too strong and unpredictable, the approach too fast. His dangling feet barely missed the lichen-covered rocks as he overshot and the stiff updraft from the far side flipped the light craft like a feather. The left wingtip caught the edge of a boulder. He spun, hit, flipped again, and cart wheeled down the slope until one wing wedged between two rocks and snapped into kindling. His body, bruised and battered, came to rest against a small, twisted bush.

He lay still for a long time in the wreck. The wind, now that he had come to rest on the ground, was obviously stronger that he had ever experienced. It was a palpable force, cold and unrelenting, and although he was chilled and wished to move and find shelter, he could not overcome the feeling that if he stood, he would be swept away over some unseen abyss.

The harness finally decided the matter. It cut into his

flesh and slowed the circulation to his arms. The wound began to throb so he made a move to relieve it, and his motions continued, as if each tentative action proved he was alive and worthy of another chance. However, his body screamed, so he slumped back onto the ground, letting it have its way momentarily as he decided where his motions should take him next.

But, gradually, the wracked glider framework and bow under his back grew too uncomfortable and he rolled to his right, favoring his bad arm as much as he could and still maintain his balance. Once on his knees, his muscles quit their complaining, as if being erect had settled them back into the positions they had desired all along. Although he stumbled as he stood, he remained on his feet and began to feel better as he moved around to shed the glider and gather his things and his wits. Besides, he began to feel the warmth creep back into his cramped extremities, and they throbbed to be on the move.

He hid the remains of the glider between some low bushes and rocks, and then climbed the short way back to the base of an outcropping to kneel by a boulder on the backbone of the ridge, trying to decide which way to go. The three ravines came together below. He could wait for them here, but he was too high and the cover too sparse. He looked for better cover and an area large enough to move around in below him. He would have to encounter them early on, much farther down the mountain where he would have room to retreat and ambush again from above if the first one did not work. But which ravine, which holds their trail? This was his immediate problem.

Then, the obvious hit him with the force of embarrassment at his own stupidity. Although it was not certain they would use the same trail both ways, the raiding party must have used one of the ravines' pathways on their trip to his village. He could look above, cut their tracks, and follow them down the slope finding the places he needed as he went. He could prepare as he closed the distance between them, becoming familiar with likely places to hide or attack as he looked for the means to pull strength out of weakness.

It did not take long. The trail was easily found on the short-grassed meadow above the ravines. It came down the incline in long, slanted diagonals, quartering the steepness at every turn. There were places where raiders had lost footing and slid a ways, and where rocks had been overturned in small avalanches. This made it difficult to read, to tell if the number going down was the same as that returning. Had they left another rear guard behind, at the base of the mountain?

It was getting late, and as he began to worry about the timing, he was struck again by his ignorance. He ducked behind two sheltering boulders, out of the wind and sight, and turned his full attention back up the trail. It was an obvious question that had been lurking behind all the others, plaguing him without ever forming itself into words.

As he sat chewing the sweet and slightly spicy meats, he could not answer it, no matter how quickly he chewed. But what intrigued him the most was that he had never, never heard the question uttered. It had never found words in his village, as far as he knew. As the wind whirled around the boulders' edges, he sent the soft words gliding down the mountainside, like bubbles on the migrant breeze.

"But, where are they going?" Indeed, it was so obvious, as was its twin: "Where are they from?" If their village is somewhere up in the mountains, he had not seen signs of it from the air. No smoke or activity.

He realized in a sinking moment that the questions flow into one another. Who are they? What do they do with their captives? Are they people, like him? Just how little he knew about his enemy, about his world, actually, beyond the narrow confines of his village and valley washed over him. He had imagined things, in the dark distance of his childhood, but to do so, he had been told, risked bringing the raiders, drawing them to his thoughts like moths to a light. He had been warned, but these mental wanderings diminished over time. There was so little information, and the stories themselves became vague or conflicting in details. And always, they stopped here, on the slopes where his people's bones might lay, bleached and unburied. Mourning family members had returned to try to claim the bodies after the painful defeats, but they, too, did not return. After the first disappeared on the mountainside, the others refused to follow, resigned to, if not completely accepting, the hopelessness of continuing.

So the knowledge of his people ended here. Perhaps the raiders were mountain beings that lived on the barren slopes above. Perhaps they lived in the emptiness beyond, in the gray area on the other side of the mountains to which Kai's imagination had never journeyed, until now. Perhaps he had made it farther than any of his people before. Maybe he would return with the unasked questions, and their answers.

The possibility intrigued him and it risked sweeping him to an imagined hero's welcome that had too many obstacles before it could become reality to make it a satisfying daydream. Convinced that no one was moving on the slopes above, he rose into the stiff wind, and turned back down toward the steep trail.

In the twilight he almost missed it. The first booby trap was unlike any trap he had seen before. He was familiar with the trip lines of snares and dead falls. He had used them all his life to catch small animals, but this was very different, so different in fact that he was amazed that he spotted it at all. It was made up of a series of small branches arranged symmetrically outward from a central shaft. In general shape, it resembled the tall flowers among the seedlings in which it stood, with the exceptions of its perfect symmetry and its bleached coloration. These two things in the odd slant of twilight captured his attention, although he had not considered the possibility of traps at all. He was moving parallel to the trail, but not on it: to do so would leave tracks. It seemed an unlikely place to put a trap, since he was so near the trail the raiders themselves would use. In a crisis, traps here would limit their own alternatives to the trail. They couldn't move off it without risk.

He stopped to examine it closely. The branches were pointed, with very small barbs slanting backwards at the end. As he looked about him, he could see other flowers and seedlings off in the distance that could be equally deadly, no doubt, and he could then see the terrible logic of their placement. He could imagine their effect on a group of people coming uphill into the unknown, the confusion and horror they could create as men moved by stealth away from the trail only to erupt into screams, or worse, fall dead without a sound.

He closed his eyes, feeling the history of his people, perhaps, or at the very least his own empathy for those who died on these slopes. Their screams were no longer vague reverberations through a story; they were a part of this forest, these winds, and him. He could feel their presence around him in the hushed murmur of the wind through the plants. The raiders had prepared well with their intricate, devious plans, but their plans seemed to work so they must feel safe and secure in this place. That, too, could be used against them. He was learning.

The raiders worked through misdirection, by antithesis. They left Kai's village on one trail, and moved to another. In the dark after their attack, someone could be easily fooled into chasing in the wrong direction and wasting valuable time. Here, they assumed that attackers would not be stupid enough to walk on the trail, but smart enough to follow it as closely as possible. They anticipated. They used logic, sometimes inverted it. The voice urged him to use that knowledge. In his head, dozens of stories about monsters and evil doings swirled, and from them all came one clear message of survival: all evil is predictable. Systematically understandable. To anticipate it is to have power, and to turn evil back upon itself is to succeed.

Taking to the trail, he picked up his pace while still keeping a wary eye on the trail's shoulders ahead and periodically stopping to listen up the trail behind him. He had a theory about how the raiders operated, but it was only that, a theory, and theories were only one step removed from confusion, chaos and collapse. Defeat.

The trail followed one side of the ravine down, staying mid-way on its left incline most of the time. At times, it dropped toward the bottom of the canyon, and then he could hear the mad rush of a small stream below him in the trees. There was ample cover along the trail when the forest began to thicken as he went farther down the slope. Above, where he had entered, all was opened and exposed.

He returned to the timberline, and on the fringe of the forest he began to make his own booby traps in the gathering dark. In a rockslide on the slope above the trail, he tried to build a dead fall using the tenuously balanced boulders, but it would not work well. Lacking materials such as twine, he tried to fashion a branch into a trip lever. It could work, but it was obvious and one would have to hit it full force to make it spring its deadly load.

He climbed the slide, looking as he went for their own booby traps. There were none, so he understood that the slide was a recent one and assumed that it had swept the hillside clean. He could use that as well. He left his own trap in place, moving away from it with little hope that it would prove useful.

He went back down the trail, moving slowly now in the dark, pacing his steps to lessen the chance he would stumble or slide. He kept his eyes on the darkness ahead, his nose constantly testing each new wisp of wind rising to him with the contours of the land. He stopped twice to rest and to eat, but mostly to slow his heart, which at times threatened to burst from his chest in a mad scream, warning all those who may be waiting. Each step seemed doomed to betray him, and the anxiety mounted as the incline lessened and he neared the point where he knew he might find them at any turn. He moved more cautiously as he progressed, but he need not have bothered.

By midnight he heard them, then saw the flicker of their campfire on the tips of the trees in the distance. He stopped dead still to listen. Above the pounding of his heart, he heard snatches of conversations, buzzings that came to him as vaguely possible, human language, but they were still too far away for words to be distinct.

Fighting every instinct he possessed, every instinct that possessed him, and every lesson he had been taught, Kai proceeded down the middle of the trail, one careful, intent step at a time. He was in no hurry, he did not have far to go, and he wanted to allow a little more time to see if they would sleep. It was late, and even if they were excited about being near their homes, they must also be very tired. He moved, stopped and listened, and then repeated the process. As he drew near, the murmurings slowly dissolved and the reflection of the fire began to dim. The acrid smell of their weapons hung on the breeze, but besides the dying crackle of the fire and the occasional flutter of a wind-stirred branch, all was silent.

Their camp was near the bottom of the ravine where it opened upon the first sweep of rolling foothills, a plateau that dropped away again toward the valley of Kai's village. They had only climbed a short ways up the steep incline before stopping near the stream to rest. From the dark trail, he could see the shadows of the bodies circling the fire pit, and he knew several things at a glance.

There were seven raiders on the ground in various positions of sleep. The twins were easy to spot near the center of the forms on his side of the fire, sleeping together again. However, even in the dim light from the fire he could make out the thong that tied them together at the ankles, and extended farther on in both directions to the wrists of raiders sleeping on either side. No matter which way the twins moved, their actions would be noticed.

The raiders were all dressed as the one he had killed, and this similarity was a momentary hindrance as he fought back the urge to vomit. Sinking to his knees, he bowed his head and gagged back the memory, and the remorse. But he looked up again, and his gaze rested on his sisters. Their safety fed his conviction, and he slowly but surely gained his feet.

Only seven. Were there guards? He had not passed the oldest battlefield, the one in the open meadow along the stream where so many were said to have died and been left unburied, so he assumed that they were above it. If this is the same trail. He would let no qualms or doubts slow him unnecessarily. Life is risk, and he felt the voice urge him forward.

As his mind raced, his eyes took in the rest of the scene, searching the far side of the darkness for movement, or places of concealment. They found a stack of firewood, instead, and he knew that this was an old camp, one often used and therefore a part of their intricate plans. The thought encouraged him. They must feel safe here, just as his own people would feel safe walking along the trail above their village. Perhaps there would be no guard, only the thong for the captives.

Guards or no guards, he prepared to enter the camp. If they were anticipating visitors, he would know soon enough, but, knowing what little he did of their thinking, he believed they would expect attack only from below, not from above. His chances were good, if they all were tired and slept soundly.

He moved between the camp and the stream to cushion his sounds with its noise, but this also made it difficult for him to use his best sense, his hearing. Still, he had the advantage, even though he could not measure their breathing as he would have liked. He would wager they were asleep, not simply waiting. He checked the arrow that had rested in his bow throughout the walk from above, and then loosened the knife in its sheath. Although the bow was once again an encumbrance, there were seven of them. Although confident, he was no fool.

The fire was almost dead by the time he finally stepped into the clearing. He paused the moment he was exposed and listened. There was no movement, no sudden flash, so he chose his way and stepped farther from the cover behind. He stepped cautiously through the prone figures, each step taking intense consideration as he controlled each detail of each minute movement of his feet and torso. He raised one foot over the body of one raider, and set it down so softly on the other side. It seemed to take forever for his foot to touch solid ground again. Thus, he made his way. Twigs, tufts of loose rock, a slight stirring of the breeze, these were the things that took his whole attention, his whole being as he scanned not only the spot where his next step would land, but also the surrounding darkness, the shadows of the trees. His ears began to ring with their effort. His scalp tingled.

It took forever, and it was only a short distance. With each step, he felt dawn approaching. The sweat began to trickle down his back, and this, too, added to his sense of urgency, battling with his will and adding to his anxiety further. The war was still waging when he came to rest at the feet of his sisters, wishing they had lain down with their heads to the trail, but they had not, perhaps because it would have helped him immensely. Then, he could have covered both their mouths at one time and roused them to help in their own escape. As it was, he could not risk stepping between them and one of their captors. Instead, he would have to cut first through the thong, and then wake them. There appeared to be ample slack in the line, so he scanned the darkness once more and then carefully put his bow down beside him, its arrow still nocked. Slipping his knife from its sheath, he gently lifted the thong.

It had an odd feel to it, light and slick, unlike the leather he was used to, but he could not wait to examine it closely. He slid the sharp blade, worn thin with use and preparation, under it and, doubling the thong, grasped it tightly for the cut. The raider to whom it was tied stirred, and then rolled partially over away from the girls, drawing the thong taut. Kai did not release his grip as the raider rolled, but pulled lightly instead. The stubborn wrist pulled back, but then relaxed and relinquished the slack Kai needed as the raider returned to his dreams.

Again he tugged with his knife. The thong held. In disbelief and growing agitation, he began a sawing action. The thong would not separate. His confusion grew. His grip tightened around the bone handle and, he realized too late, on the thong itself. His sister stirred, rolled over, and gasped. She was unable to stifle her surprise and he was too slow to reach her mouth before the air had escaped and the damage done. The raider, already uncomfortable and slightly troubled by the strain of the line tied to his wrist, stirred.

Kai reached for the bow at his feet and the string was taut before the raider rolled to his feet, away from Kai. The thong tripped him up as he reached for his weapon and Kai's sister complicated his dilemma by tugging to keep his bound hand inconsequential. The device meant to control and trap had been turned against him, but the comical scene was short lived as the arrow took him directly in the chest . . . and fell harmlessly to the ground. The force of the blow, however, was enough to stun the raider momentarily, and Kai, recovering quickly from his confusion over the defective arrow, lunged forward, knocking the raider down under him. So far, the encounter had been quiet, there had been no time to raise the alarm, and Kai had his knife in hand again.

The raider struggled, and under him Kai could feel her form. The knife hung still for the briefest part of a heartbeat as Kai's confusion diverted him, but it was time enough. She hit him in the side with something hard, and the old wound came back to haunt him. He brought the knife down, handle butt first, hard against her temple. She gave a brief, pain-filled sigh, but it was loud enough to give the alarm.

He scooped up the bow as he rose and jumped toward

the trail, half stooped, and into the darkness. Something came up, and he nocked another arrow on the move. A raider was rising near the trail, and as he came erect, Kai shot. The arrow hit him in the throat. He had aimed for the eyes but the effect was nonetheless worthwhile as the raider doubled over in a fit of gagging. There was a flash as Kai reached the path, but the blast from the fire weapon went wide, striking a tree ahead of him and to the right. It burst into smoke and red cinder.

Kai feigned to the left, down the trail, then plunged into the dark ravine toward the stream. It worked. There were two more flashes in quick succession on the trail as he disappeared into the tangle of brush along the streambed. The raiders' night vision worked in his favor it seemed. The weapons' flashes had blinded them.

He did not slow down, despite the sharp incline and the thorns and unforgiving branches and the nagging thought of booby traps. At this moment, when his personal safety was in question for the third time of his life, he sacrificed the comfort of his parts to the good of his whole. The pain that registered in the crunch of the moment was of no consequence, and even the unknown so closely in front of him could not match his fear of what was behind.

He did not slow down once his feet found water, but moved out into the middle of the streambed, stumbling his way into the roar and drag of the current. It would take precious time for them to reach the lip of the canyon. They had no way of knowing which direction he had come or which way he would go. They must assume what, for them, would be the obvious. They would reason, and this meant they would think downstream, toward his people. This gave him time.

He scrambled up a large boulder and began the climb, jumping from rock to rock up the canyon until he thought his lungs would burst. The streambed was steep, steeper than the trail. The water fell in short, sudden drops over and around the huge, sometimes jagged boulders that were his path. At times he was forced to climb down, and then up again, making his way even farther. His bare knees became raw and bled, and his hands ached, but he was alive and he had a direction, and a plan.

Dawn was approaching. First, the thick darkness began to soften, and then came the seeping cold, the grayness that marked the return of vision. Kai waited. He was terribly tired, played out, but he waited silently, motionlessly. It had been a hard, impossible climb, but he had made it with time to spare. Not trusting the ravine's incline near the trail, despite his certainty about raider logic and not daring the steeper rock formations on the far side of the stream, he had climbed the river bed all the way, rock by rock, to the slide.

There, he climbed rock again, to the trail and then above it. He had failed at rescuing his sisters and the raiders would be on full alert, so for the moment he was content to slow, perhaps even stop, the raiding party's escape, giving his people time to catch up with them. Then, he would try the streambed once again, this time down, to tell his people what he had learned about booby traps off the trail, the weapons, the impenetrable clothes, the trail ahead, the woman who is one of them. Perhaps he'd know more by then.

And Kai waited. The thoughts of potential failure and uncertain futures were his only company. He was too tired to think of anything else, too weary to let his mind slip from this one imperative of confrontation. He had no hopes, except that of one simple requirement: that his sisters would be, as he imagined, in the middle of the party and that they would not appear first in the trail below him. His expectations were small, and they were met. His luck held. He did not flinch. Only his eyes followed the first raider making his tentative way up the trail, then the second, the third. Like a cat ignoring a mouse with all his attention, Kai sat perfectly still.

They had their fire weapons drawn and all of them moved slowly, watching the trees below the trail and intently scanning the streambed whenever it appeared through the trees. They leaned one way, and then another, and then moved slowly forward. They were looking for him. They were focused, attentive, but not on all their surroundings, only the stream. By the time first one stepped over the first wave of rocks on the edge of the slide, then stopped to look to the remaining pile of rocks in front of him, and then turned his steady gaze up the hillside, Kai had already sprung the trap.

The avalanche came down too quickly for the raider to even find his footing in the rocks and gravel. There was no time to react, only wonder. The two raiders behind him had no time to move before they were swept away in rock and dirt and brush and boulders that came in a wave of rolling fury. The one in the rear was flung backwards to do a brief, comical dance step on the loose ground, and then to disappear over the lip of the canyon.

It came down too quickly and unpredictably and Kai, unused to the ways of rolling rocks and debris and mountains, came down with it. Although he managed to leap free of the boulders behind which he hid, and the smaller one on which he stood, the ground around him was too soft, unsettled, and it began to slip downward, gaining speed. Smaller stones pummeled him; the soil threatened to bury him. He rolled to his right, away from the larger rocks and the center of the slide.

As he neared the level of the trial, he exerted his last reserve of will, rolling over an uprooted bush, scrambling against the force of the flow, praying there were no hidden booby traps near him. He slowed near the periphery of the avalanche, and then came to rest on the trail itself, but only momentarily. The slide did not slow. On his hands and knees, he scrambled once more against the momentum of the loose soil going away into the canyon. As he regained the trail's level, he began to rise to his feet against the incline, and was struck by the topmost branch of a tree making its own way toward the stream. Fortunately, it spun him around, to fall face first onto the trail's lip away from the slide's movement. His hands searched for a hold, found it, gripped and he held on with all his might.

The wind knocked from him, he lay still for a long time until the silence returned, broken only periodically by the last ripples of small rocks or dirt searching for equilibrium, their angle of repose. His legs were buried under dirt. As he looked down to them, he could see below him small bushes and here and there a large tree, dislodged and deposited into odd designs and arrangements in the canyon below the trail. His ears ringed, and at first he could not hear the stream. Pulling free, halfway digging his legs out with one hand while the other maintained its grip, he began his crawl once more to the trail.

Sitting on its edge, he looked around at chaos. The slide would make it much more difficult for the raiders to escape, but not impossible. Below, it had blocked the stream, forming a dam behind which the waters grew. This would give them pause. They would have to risk the loose climb along the old trail, and that would worry them.

His bow, quiver and pack were gone. There was no sign of the first two raiders. The third, however, was only a short distance down the hill. He had been stopped by two trees, and lay at their bases with his back carelessly draped along the curvature of one trunk, his feet uphill. Kai could not tell if he was dead or merely unconscious. There was no movement, and with his ears ringing, Kai was virtually deaf. But his heart gave a jump, and his hopes followed.

There, three body lengths from the raider, a bright glimmer in the growing dawn light. It was one of their weapons, and a new plan began to take form and substance from that bright reflection. For the first time, the impossible seemed possible, then plausible and perhaps probable. With a weapon, and with three more raiders out of the way, perhaps another wounded back near the camp, coming from behind . . .

Kai rose to his knees. His ears rang. As his foot came up under him to push him erect, the blow came as too much a surprise for his mind to register it. There, simply, was the hillside, and then, utter and total darkness.

Chapter Five
# Burial

Kai awoke into darkness so profound he wondered if he might be dead. Maybe this is what it feels like, he thought. Fortunately, there was the pain in his head—not a throb, really, but a dull and constant ache with a sharp edge that grew beyond the hope of relief—and it slowly convinced him he was, in fact, alive. He believed his eyes were open. He could blink, so he doubted his vision and thought that he might have gone blind.

He told his hands to explore. First, they groped for his head, finding, and then slowly examining the swollen lump of the contusion low on the back of his skull. As he gingerly probed it with cautious fingertips, he tried to remember where he had gotten it. He also tried to probe behind this intense darkness to the time before, and as he tried to reconstruct events, he felt even more confused. Where was he? If he was dead, did pain go with us into that realm? If blind, as it now seemed, was he alone? He let his hands take their time back to his sides. How long had he been out? And who hit him?

His hands took to exploring the surroundings within their reach as his other senses came to life, sending out their own queries. In the background he could hear a dull, deep humming sound, and occasionally sharper, short-lived and distant sounds he could not make out. Nothing was familiar, not even the smells that slowly forced their way into his mind, where the voice was completely silent. All the senses were disjointed and the sounds had no rhythm to them that would tell him what they were or how they fit into his world.

Then he thought of his family and all the last few days came rushing back, including the last image: the slide, the weapon, the stream, the raider's body draped over the debris. His confused senses told him the ugly truth. He was no longer in his world.

His hands, groping through his blindness, found only smooth, cold, angular and hard surfaces, as unfamiliar in their shapes as the materials out of which they were constructed. He was lying on his back on a flat, hard slab. Stone? Its edges were sharp and squared off as he gripped for a hold to help him sit up but his grip slipped, dropping him back with a grunt.

He tried again and as he rose, the ordeals of the last few days came heavily upon him and he wished with all his might that he would wake up from this crazy dream with his sisters giving him grief for sleeping in. Then he could just lie back down and sleep secure in the comfort that he would awake once more into a world full of order and sympathy and people and futures painted on smiling faces.

But his muscles were cramped and sore and they refused any proposal to lay back on the rock slab to sleep or do anything else. How long had he been out? It was as he stretched his aching muscles that he found a wrapping on his wounded arm. Exploring once more by feel he found another patch of similar material on the smaller burn under his armpit, held there by some sort of strap. He probed them both, gently but thoroughly.

The contact brought back the memory of the discomfort he had ignored for the last days, but there was no immediate pain from his wounds. Instead, there was a dull numbness. Even the scrape on his back from the collapse of the holy Shelter had been tended to, but it was not covered like the others. The bump on the back of his head had a sticky substance, too. He smelled his fingers after dabbing them on the wound again. It did not bring the rusty flavor to the back of his tongue, so it was not blood. The contradictions, the conflicts of senses began to build into a confusion frightening in its power. Someone had taken care of him. Someone had brought him here. But where? To look after his wounds. Why? The same man that had tried to crush his skull? Did someone tend wounds of the dead?

Raiders. He was in grave danger. Their lack of mercy, their inhuman, savage acts were both the substance of story and now his own experience. He had to escape.

He swung his legs over the edge of the slab. He had always prided himself on his vision, and now in this total absence of light or reflection he felt useless, and too, too vulnerable. The slab may be close to the ground; it may be high, high over a pit. He had no way of knowing. So, sending out what feelers he could, he assumed the best but took the precaution of going over backwards, lowering himself a bit at a time using his forearms and elbows to brace his weight against the rock slab. His toes, dropping into the darkness below, made contact.

There was a dazzling flash. His eyes snapped instinctively shut as his mind prepared for the searing pain from the weapon's blast. His arms faltered, and then gave way and he slammed into the hard, inflexible ground, rolling by instinct, searching for the small comfort of shelter under the slab.

Once there he could tell, even through his clinched eyelids, that the flash was not a weapon but a constant, unyielding glare. Under the shade of the slab, however, he was able to sit in a hunched position to rub his eyes, trying to free them of the tears that would not stop flowing. Between rubbings, he was able to take brief, painful glimpses through defiant eyelids of his blurred surroundings. The light was pervasive, unrelenting, but he was thankful that it was not the flash of the weapon that he feared.

He was in a room, but unlike any room he had ever seen. The walls were flat, smooth, uniform and came together perfectly in the corners. This one characteristic fascinated him to distraction.

Slowly drawing himself out from under his scanty shelter, he took it all in with a slow, cautious sweep, circling on his heels. Each scene added to his confusion, and his dilemma. A small room. No windows. And only one door, directly in front of him as he finished his circuit facing in the direction he had begun it. Besides the slab, there was a small table, a bench growing out of the wall itself, and he fought back the urge to forget everything else to examine how it did this. It had no legs. Besides these things, the room was completely bare, hard, impersonal.

And a sudden understanding struck him. He could not

feel others around him and this worried him a great deal. Never in his life, even in the valley below and on the trail toward the mountains to save his sisters, had he moved without the sure feel of others in his soul. This absence made him dizzy, adding to his disorientation. The word monsters came back to him and he started to shake.

He took a few tentative steps, only to slump back once more against the slab. The bright light came from directly above him so he leaned back to look up at this new wonder. It was too close, too bright. It hurt his eyes, but he could make out a ring around it. This odd and alien enclosure, these strange and inconceivable things proved too much for someone battered and confused and lost. His head began to swim and, again dizzy, he pulled himself back onto the slab to recapture his strength.

The light went away and the total darkness came in less that the blinking of an eye. He blinked, and when his eyes opened he was blind again. His scalp began to tingle and he could feel the sweat begin to form along his temples and on the under sides of his arms. In this terrible disjointed confusion, he dropped once again to feel solid ground beneath his feet.

And the light came back in all its blinding intensity. He began to experiment. First, he climbed back onto the slab, no light, back to the floor, light. His fascination was uncontrollable. He did it again and again, forgetting his driving need to get free, to free his sisters, and during this odd flashing from dark to light, the odd confusion of sun and ground, the door opened.

Kai stared at a vision before him. It was a human. It was

more than human. His shock shook him to the core as the questions roared back in: who had brought him here and why? He could understand why the raiders would capture him— they'd want revenge—but was this beautiful image standing in the doorway a raider, or another of their captives?

She was young, like him, perhaps a bit older. He could not tell for certain, so devoid was she of those visible traits that marked the age of people in his village: the wrinkles and scars and signs of life. She wore a long, flowing garment over a skirt that ended just above her knees. It was light, bright in color unlike those of the women he knew, and it waved in motion constantly echoing her own movements as she entered the room, and this told him that it was soft and pliant but made of a foreign material. His gaze dropped down her legs to her feet, which were not bare as his own, but strapped to some thick under soles with a contrivance that reminded him remotely of the lashings he had used for his glider. They looked uncomfortable, and then he thought of the tracks on the trail. She did not seem to be alarmed by his close scrutiny, or by the ways that his muscles tensed at the thought of the raiders.

She noticed the subtle shift in his thoughts, he could feel it, but her smile remained steady, lighting her slender face and dark, curious eyes framed by the soft, shoulder-length sweep of dark, dark hair. She raised her hands, as if to show him that she held no weapons, but he had already determined this and did not respond to her gesture. Instead, he winced at the sight of her delicate arms as her sleeves fell away. They intrigued him. They made him feel odd, but he could not tell why for certain. He relaxed, just a bit.

"You must be wondering where you are." He covered his surprise too slowly, and his response was a garbled, poorly constructed and half-finished blurb that, mercifully, was allowed to die a graceful death in her steady, open smile. She had spoken as his people speak, with the same words, and she looked as they did, but the stories of his youth told of the raiders' odd speech. He was unprepared to understand. Was she a raider or not? He was ignorant and did as he had been taught from his earliest lessons: he remained dumb to learn.

She moved into the room, and before he could look behind her to see what was outside, the door blew quietly back into its place, latching with a distinct click. Moving around her, he looked but could not see a latch, a thong to open it, and it was obviously tightly fitted into the frame. He had missed a chance to escape, and now he did not want to reveal his ignorance, his weakness. Taking a deep breath without letting his chest noticeably expand, he turned back ready to face what was to come.

"You don't need to be afraid, you know." She had seated herself on the low bench and drawn her feet back up on it, her slender arms wrapped casually around her knees. "We won't hurt you." The words were familiar, but the way she used them was different. He caught her meaning fully and blanched a bit despite his attempt at control. To suggest that he would be frightened of them, or her, stung his ego, but he held his tongue and guarded his facial muscles.

"Ah, you are proud I see." She looked down to the floor and withdrew slightly from that openness so profound only a breath before. "I'm not supposed to be here. We're not

supposed to talk to you people until you've been educated."
The last implication was too much, and although still in
control, his eyes flashed his hot hate. So, these were indeed
the raiders, those who took his people at their will. Teach-
ers? Crap, he thought. Pure crap.

"Oh, I'm sorry. You didn't understand. I meant, after your
orientation. You will be treated well, but you have to learn
about us before you can understand." Her smile returned,
wholly sincere, wholly friendly.

"Do all your prisoners understand?" He gave her only time
enough to recoil. "Who are you? And where am I? You can
begin my lessons now." But his voice had an edge to it, a
harshness despite his inner voice, which cautioned him to
be careful. However, as his lips moved, there came into his
words a thinly veiled hint of scorn, so her smile disappeared.

"I hoped we'd be friends. You're the first young boy in a
long, long time. Maybe the first ever. I don't know." His
eyes betrayed him again. True, he was uninitiated; true he
was young; but he was not a boy. No longer a boy. Could a
boy make her people pay? Could a boy have gotten this far?
But his thoughts were blocked from saying these words by
the dark resigned eyes of a dying raider, behind him on a
hill, and by the lump on the back of his head that finally
began to throb as if to warn him about excessive pride, im-
pulsive actions and their costs. He had not been successful,
only lucky for a while.

She got up and went to the door where she paused briefly
and then touched a raised square near its outer edge. The
door sprung open and she stepped out. "My father will be
here soon to talk with you. If you need anything, or you

choose to be friendly, just ask for me. My name is Ursla." She turned to her left and disappeared behind the doorframe, leaving only the framed section of a brightly lit, shallow room, its walls identical to those in his own. The door hissed and clicked back into place. He did not need to stop it now. He had watched her actions closely. He could open it after he prepared to make a run for it, before her father arrived. Surely there were guards outside. He would need a weapon, but the room was empty.

It didn't take long for him to decide that he would have to face them unarmed. The table, slab, and bench were heavy and fastened down by a method he did not understand. They appeared unbreakable, even if he were fortunate enough to have a tool to use on them. There was nothing, not even a remote possibility of a weapon, so he removed his leather shirt, chewing and ripping two rawhide thongs from it that had been used to stitch it together. Knotted together, they formed a crude noose. He knotted it again in the middle, and taking a series of deep breaths and muttering a quick but heartfelt prayer, he went to the door.

He was still trying to open it a long while later when it opened on its own to reveal an older man with a dignified look about him, despite his apparent shock at finding himself nose to nose with a young man with a noose.

Kai's surprise and confusion drew the man's attention from the thong, and then to the obvious. "Well, if you're going to try to throttle me, at least get on with it and do a good job." Although Kai did not understand, he could fully appreciate the implications in the other's tone. He let the thong disappear behind a thigh, but he did not loose his grip on it.

"Well, I hope that's a step in the right direction. My name is Lorn and I have been instructed to take care of you myself, although I must admit I don't know why. Anyway, we will be spending a lot of time together, so I had hoped you would begin by trusting me. We will not hurt you. We want to help you."

He moved a step closer, his right hand raised as if to touch Kai's shoulder. Without giving up ground, the boy rolled his shoulder away, his hand gripping the noose even tighter. If he only knew the secret of the door, which had clicked shut again with the old man's movements. "I just want to check your bandages. Do your wounds trouble you?"

He took Kai's silence as a sign that he needed no immediate treatment. "Well, let's go for a walk, shall we? But first, let me establish one necessary point. I see that you are a violent person and that you act impulsively. We'll get along well, if you keep in mind that you are our guest. It would be good of you to act like one."

Kai studied the man's wrinkled face, the gray hairs on his temples, his dark and unrevealing eyes. He thought of Luther and searched for the real meanings behind words, growing increasingly impatient with his situation. The old man implied a lot, and one of the things was that he was defenseless and had to obey. Kai did not like to play by rules.

"Guests can leave when they choose."

The man chuckled. "Yes. Yes. Yes. Of course, all in good time. That will come. All we ask is to be heard first, a chance for you to understand us: the way we live and the way we are. Once we have shown you, you can return to your people, if you still wish to." The boy's obvious surprise was not lost on him. "We're not savages, after all. We treasure human life and individual worth." And the boy's opposite reaction was quickly noted and recorded with equal precision.

"I wish to return to my people, now. They need me now." The man looked increasingly uncomfortable. "How long have I been here?"

But he paused only briefly before he answered. "Only a short time, actually." But there was no response, so he elaborated. "A day. You were obviously in a wasted condition, so we kept you at rest. It was for the best, you see." The boy stared blankly back at him.

Lorn had not worked with these people for years, and now, after all this time, to be called back to it was illogical. It didn't make any sense. He had forgotten the difficulties it involved, the intricacies of their thought processes, the deficiencies of their language and ideas. "For a day we kept you asleep."

Kai's agitation grew noticeable. How far had Luther and the others come? Was it too late to avoid the slaughter? But his restlessness was met by an equal agitation on the part of his inquisitor, who seemed eager to avoid some topics and to be out of the confines of this small, cramped room with a boy who obviously wanted to do him harm. "Let's go for a walk, shall we?"

"First, I want to know about my people. Have they attacked?" The older man scrutinized him even closer. He was beginning to develop a seed of respect for this boy who had come farther than any of his kind before. He was ingenious, inventive, and therefore potentially useful, but dangerous.

He was also forthright, direct, and if he answered him, Lorn would have to reveal that, indeed, he was being held captive by his sworn enemies. He would also have to admit that he knew this boy's people were on their way, and what would happen when they arrived on the mountain's slopes. But his hesitation was brief. "They have not appeared. Perhaps, this time, they won't." He moved toward the door. Give them quick responses, and show as little concern as possible, and they take it for truth, the lack of emotion a sure sign of an indifference born out of strength, and strength is truth for these creatures.

At the door, he paused to let the boy prepare. He would watch this one closely, indeed. Surveillance had missed his landing and the remains of the glider until too late. The tech responsible had already been transferred to another operation, but a glider! This was the interesting part. It had been so long.

Actually, it was probably best that they had missed him at first. The search for him had proven quite instructive. A full, realistic check of their defenses had never been made because it had never been required. The first recognition of the wreckage had been followed by a successful, clear image that made it easy to identify the device with existing historical records. But they were so involved with that process that they made their first operational error.

They had sequenced scans uphill, assuming the intruder was bent upon infiltration. The logic of this defense was irreversible until hours later as they re-tuned and refined and re-calibrated, thinking their scanners at fault for not spotting him. By then, they were too late. It was the hurried signal from the party below that finally got the scanners turned in the right quadrant, spotting him with infrared but losing him again in the slide where the sensors had been destroyed. It had been quite instructive, this cat and mouse game with a boy who could make advantage out of nothing.

"Come, let's walk. There's plenty of time. Your people won't attack. Once they get to the old battleground they'll reconsider, then turn home. We have all learned things since that first violent encounter. They will come; they will return home. It's the only logical thing to do. Besides, it's been done before, so don't worry about them. Come, let me show you around."

Kai thought to contest this man's view of his people and of history, but was stopped by the opening of the door. It hissed wide at the slightest touch from the man's fingers on the raised square. Dumbfounded, angry and distracted by his own failure to open it, Kai was not prepared for what met him beyond.

Although accustomed to the bright light of his room, he was taken back by the glare outside it. It was not more intense, only equally bright. What made it different was that it revealed and accentuated the visual shock as he stepped into not another, smaller room as he had thought, but a long, long narrow way extending in two directions to left and right, enclosed in walls and roof. The discrepancy between what he had expected and the scope and magnitude of what he encountered shook him for a moment, knocking him off balance. But the light. Even as he tried to see to the end of the way to his right, he could tell that the light did not falter nor waver in the vast distance, but was constantly and equally present at all places on its path. There were no shadows.

While he struggled to take this in, he noted that there were no guards. He looked around. There were no places where a guard could hide, only smooth hard walls converging in the distance. Periodically, people seemingly materialized on one side, passed across in brief flashes, only to disappear from view in the other. They were there, and then they were gone, and this occurred again and again at varying distances. But then also sudden flickers of movements in similar crossings, but not people. He straightened his backbone. He was in for difficult times with so many foreign things coming at him. He would not be overwhelmed by the new and unfamiliar.

"This way."

As they moved off, there was a slight disturbance behind them and Kai stepped instinctively to the wall while pivoting at the waist to face whoever was silently approaching. What he encountered, he could not tell, but it had come suddenly and quickly and now it rested behind them, humming. Lorn seemed unconcerned, almost oblivious to its presence, so Kai tried to mimic his ease. "Of course, we could ride, if you prefer?" Since his outstretched hand indicated what looked like benches on the sides of the thing, Kai could infer his offer. He did not want to touch the thing, so he shook his head, a bit too stiffly he thought. Lorn simply turned back in the direction they had begun, and the squat craft whirred past them and disappeared in the distance. "I'm glad. I like to walk and I just seem never to have the time any more."

Their course took no direct path, but turned suddenly in squared angles only to enter an identical pathway in another direction. Kai began to doubt his ability to retrace his way back to the room, so unfamiliar was this left, right, right, left wandering. But then, he did not want to go back there, only back to his people. This required that he be patient and learn how to accomplish one, overriding goal. To get out of this building. He was content to absorb and wonder quietly. Lorn accommodated him because he did not cease in his chatter.

At first, Kai tried to pay close attention, but as they stopped before one great whirring thing much like the others the man had enthusiastically waved at from time to time during their walk, and as he quickly dropped words like unfamiliar animals to crawl around in Kai's head to perplex and mystify, trying to explain but only confusing Kai more until all his speech became nonsensical, Kai concentrated not on them or the thing before them, but upon the rise and fall of the pitch and timbre, the sounds around him. Lorn's voice was only one small, fragmented piece of all the conflicting noises. He tried, at first, to understand, but gave up as understanding drew further and further away. He had never heard such clatter.

So, he walked in silence until Lorn, himself, came to understand. "I'm sorry. I guess I am too eager, too proud. I should wait until later, until you've begun your orientation and have the fundamentals. But, we are almost there."

"Where?"

"The Center. All will be explained."

They walked farther. "I have never seen a house so large.

How can it stand? And why have my people not spoken of it?"

Absentmindedly, Lorn mumbled his answer as they turned yet another corner. "House? Mmm. Sort of, I imagine. But they did know of it, once."

Kai would, in the normal course of things, have pressed him further, and wanted to badly, but as they turned into a short, dimmer passage, he caught some variation out of the corner of his eye as he looked to Lorn. The passages before had been impressive but as he directed his attention in front of them, what he saw struck him immobile and completely dumb.

At first, he believed they were finally stepping out of the house and into the mountains, a valley perhaps. The vista before him opened into a wide sweep in which the light shone brightly down upon a collection of tall, radiantly white houses such as he had never seen. Their size alone stunned and humbled him. They rose into the sky like giant trees, but they were not, and the sky had a bright light shining down. He looked to Lorn, but then immediately back to the scene in front of him.

Something was wrong, although everything was beautiful, orderly, clean. Rows of windows and doorways appeared along the ways, trees lined long walks, and shrubs could be seen not just at ground level, but also above him. The tall houses once again drew his attention up their trunks and into the sky. Something was wrong here.

The movements of people near him brought him back, and he noticed for the first time that there were people, lots of people, everywhere, moving not in haste but casually.

Even at this, Kai felt dizzy with the rush of new sensations, the disorientation of his perception, and he slumped back against the wall to steady himself. There were familiar things here—people, trees, grass—but he did not know them. His confusion mounted, and it grew as he slowly sent his senses outward to unravel this scene, this anomaly.

Lorn had continued on and it was a moment before he realized that he was walking alone. Stopping, he looked back in Kai's direction for a moment before returning with a quizzical look. "Are you all right?" And when he was not answered immediately he took in the crisis at one swallow, catching Kai by the elbow just in time before he slumped to the ground.

And with this touch, Kai understood. It answered so many nagging questions, validated the old stories. The opacity to the sky, the stillness of the breeze. "We're still inside!"

Lorn looked around him, as if he, too, were only now— once the idea had been uttered—beginning to comprehend the obvious for the very first time. Then his face clouded. "I am truly sorry. You see, you came as a surprise. There was no time to prepare. We . . ." but his voice trailed off, leaving only a suggestive, impotent wave of his left hand to encompass all that lay around them, and all that it implied.

"We have a process, a system we use, outside, to bring in you people, but you were a surprise, and you were hurt, we didn't want to risk losing you and we did not consider well. We were hasty." Shaking his head, he steered Kai to a low bench near a group of stunted trees. The grass below their feet was stiff and ungiving, but it was dark green and alive, as were the trees. Slumping down and leaning back against the soft cushion behind, he looked to Lorn with a dull plea.

"Of course. You are correct. We are inside. Inside the mountains."

Chapter Six

# Shifting Worlds

Lorn did not continue right away but instead let the idea penetrate slowly through Kai's confusion. It would be best not to rush with this one, not to push. Lorn was not used to such resistance, so other methods would be necessary. However, this one appeared to have a rudimentary intelligence, so in time he would automatically, naturally come around. He had no other choice.

For Kai, the world had suddenly crumbled. All of that, back there—the mother asleep in their home, the uncle whose touch sent shivers of power through him, the village itself and the mountains—had shifted subtly into a larger scheme of things that contained a people and place hidden right in plain sight. He knew instinctively that his world would never be the same, that in the time it took to blink, his past and his future had altered irrevocably. He would never see his home again, at least not in the ways he saw it when he had shouldered his things and climbed the hill to fly away from it forever. He knew this without being told, and the voice in his head echoed it in a whisper.

He felt a deep sense of loss, so deep it was dull and foreboding, so deep it could not ignore the next sensations that

raced in with a power not to be denied, for the world began
to reconstruct itself immediately out of the rubble, and
with greater vision, with greater dimension and scope. The
scale had changed.

Here, the mountains that had shadowed his life from his
earliest memory, that could be seen in the blue haze from
his village, hid a race of people who had powers beyond his
wildest imagination. And his people were ignorant of them;
they had never guessed. All they knew was that, periodically,
raiders came. They knew this one fact: the raiders would
come, someone would be carried off, and others would die
trying to get the lost ones back. Who? Why? Where? These
questions, if his people even considered them, did not matter much to them; only the lost ones mattered. And for Kai
at this moment of fundamental shifting worlds, these questions had no answers.

But, these are people, like us, he thought as he looked at
Lorn. They have our shapes, our words. They must have our
feelings, too. They must share the same love of life, the love
of one another, like we do. But then he thought of the
burned homes, the shattered holy place, the lost sisters, the
deadly booby traps on the mountainside covered with
bones. There was much to be explained, and much to understand. He needed answers, and being young and used to
direct answers, he resorted to directness.

"Why do you raid our villages? Why do you take our people against their will, as prisoners?"

Lorn marveled again at this boy's frankness, his complete
lack of intimidation. Such an openness, such inquisitiveness
may help him adjust, he thought, and therefore Lorn must

keep it alive, feed bits and pieces for each hunger. If his curiosity remained active, he would prove easier to control because he would not be focused on the past, and could, therefore, be directed to the future, his future.

And he was responsive, too, quick to recoup his balance. Only a few moments ago, he had been given a shattering blow, and now he has worked through it and begun to ask questions, but not the obvious or the immediate kind. Of course, everything he had seen since he woke up had been new, completely alien to his experience. His people live in a primitive state. They have no technology to speak of. They live in a hodgepodge collection of thrown-together huts carved out of the land they barely draw a life of squalor from, and does he ask about all that he sees here? The structure itself, the transport that obviously frightened him out of his wits when he came out of the infirmary? Hardly. He strikes to the heart of the matter.

He would have to handle this one carefully, without appearing to manipulate him. Lorn made mental notes as he progressed through his analysis, and these he would transcribe for the boy's file as soon as he could find the time alone. "All that will be explained, believe me, in due time, but let me tell you this. Absolutely no one here is a prisoner. Your people stay because they want to, not because they have to."

Kai scrutinized the man's face carefully. If he would have told him that trees could fly or that hearts did not feel, he would not have been as incredulous as with this simple, impossible statement. But there was no hint of deception; Lorn's face reflected only sincerity and conviction. Kai wanted to touch him, to be sure, to verify with the feeling, but he withheld his hand. Either the man was a skillful liar, or he believed what he said. Either way, Kai would find out for himself. Men sometimes believed wrong things, things that did not prove out in lives. He must find some of his people and speak with them. "Can I see them, talk with them?" He expected to be told "all in good time" again, and in a way, hoped it so that he would have time to regroup and control his thoughts, which were hopping from one thing to another on their own.

"Of course. In fact, we're on our way to meet with two of them, but we are early. We have time to sit and rest while they get ready."

Kai leaned back into the comfort of the bench. Unwittingly, he had grown straight and stiff as he talked and his actions may have revealed his mind, so he relaxed and tried to recompose himself. He took several deep, but unhurried, breaths. Could he be waiting to see his sisters? Would they let him talk with them? It would be hard to understand, but he held a ray of hope that he might be allowed to stay with them. That would make things easier.

He took another deep breath. The air was not right. It had a stale edge to it, a dull, lifeless quality that gave him his first tremor of claustrophobia. He suddenly realized the crush of dirt and rock immediately above his head and his gaze titled in that direction, as if he half expected to see the first grains of catastrophe beginning to fall. His shoulder throbbed. He knew what it felt like to have the ceiling fall in on him.

The sense lasted only briefly. It was displaced by a new,

powerful wonder that had momentarily escaped him. There it was. The daylight and its source. It was perfectly rounded and bright and he could feel the waves of warmth seep into his face. Yet how could this be? He looked to Lorn, his sudden motion drawing the man back from his own thoughts to follow Kai's questioning gaze turned once more upward. At first, he looked back with a quizzical expression of his own, as if not understanding Kai's unspoken question, then his face cleared as it dawned on him.

"Of course! You see, it's always there, so we easily forget what an engineering masterpiece it really is." Kai's face reflected his lack of comprehension. "It's not really a sun, you see, it's an artificially created illusion. It's like a bright light that is automatically controlled to simulate the intensity of radiation for the sun at any specific time of the day. Of course, it does not move, actually, but it does 'set' at evening and 'rise' in the morning. Our ancestors thought of everything."

Then, he caught himself and stopped short. He was revealing too much, too soon, so he drew quiet and reflective, hoping to avoid any other questions. When Kai fidgeted next to him, he rose. "We should move along. Come on, let's go inside. They should be nearly ready for us now."

Unsatisfied, Kai took one more long look at the thing above, the sun Lorn called it, then rose also. Kai knew he had been dismissed, so he did not press the issue. To do so would prove useless and reveal his interests. However, he would find out more about this sun, and these ancestors.

As they walked toward the tall, angular structures at the center of the huge cave, Kai began to slow to study them more carefully. Unlike the buildings he was used to, these were smooth, like the walls of the passageway they had followed to get here, and uniform, with windows symmetrical and perfectly placed. Like everything around him, they were clean, neat, orderly. And big. They were very, very tall, rising to touch the sky, it seemed as he looked up, and the illusion increased as they drew nearer. Craning his neck to see the topmost levels, he had the sudden feeling that they were about to burst into flame and topple over upon him. The impression came so suddenly and fully that his body seemed to retreat instinctively, repulsed strongly by its innate desire for survival.

His mind became a funnel. He did not attempt to control the images, but merely swallow them as they came unasked out of the past. His knees buckled and without feeling the impact, without once even blinking, Kai fell. He realized that he was lying on the ground on his back. His body began to relax so his mind was fully free to spin through the rush of sensual associations. The intensity of the heat. The piercing screams. The dark shapes about him. The woman and her child. The images came in an intense impact, and then retreated as quickly into the pain of a memory as the startled face of Lorn appeared above him, like an ashen and slack-jawed sun.

"Are you all right? What happened? What's this, a fit?" His questions came all at once. There was no silence to fill with an answer, but Kai was not ready to answer, only ask, although he already suspected.

"Your ancestors, yours and mine, they are the same. We're related."

If Kai's fall took Lorn by complete surprise, his question shocked him into complete befuddlement. To cover his surprise, he helped the boy stand. He could not answer, trying instead to look beyond the boy's face. Conceivably, one of the savages could reach this conclusion on her own. After the battle dress of the raiding parties had been put aside to reveal the similarities of body and their words and similarities of speech were apparent, perhaps, then, one of them could draw the logical conclusions.

But no one had before. No one had even heard the possibility in a story or word, so Lorn had been sure that no one remembered. The split, the schism had been so complete and irreversible for them, and it had been so thoroughly reinforced generation after generation, that for this boy's people the raiders had become not people, but personifications of evil forces in the world beyond comprehension. To think of them as human alone was a gigantic leap, so careful were Lorn's people instructed about the conditions of contact. To make that leap to kinship status was impossible. But, he thought, this boy stands here before me and knows. The answer will simply confirm the fact. "Yes, son, we share a common ancestry."

The voice in Kai's head came to life. "There. It's done. It was a powerful expression of confirmation."

Once again, Lorn felt the control of the boy's orientation slipping from him. Already he had ruined some of the major shaping powers of the program, the revelations meant to be placed strategically in the education of the savages to shock them into awe and then appreciation followed by submission to their new world. This could be troublesome, he thought. "Come. We must go in."

Kai moved through the opening, this time without look-ing up. He allowed himself to be directed into a tiny room. The door slid closed behind them. Since Lorn turned to face it, Kai did as well, but although his body responded to the need for movement, his mind was elsewhere, racing, so he was knocked not only off balance, but back to the mo-ment by a giddy sense of rapid motion. He shifted his weight to compensate, and then looked to the old man, equally lost in thought. However, he answered without the question, and without turning to look at Kai. "We're going up. Don't worry." But Kai was not worried, only curious. If Lorn did not show fear, he would not be frightened either, and this conclusion, this acceptance of things as they were for those around him, began the process.

For the time being, he needed to think, to unravel things. Out there, at home, he had not been allowed to ask about the raiders or even about his people's past, and now he did not know if he should, if he even really wanted to know, but if they shared a past, they shared that memory of hor-rifying destruction by fire and collapse as well that he had seen in the fire. Luther had lived his whole life, almost, with that image in his head without knowing if it was also a part of the raiders' history. Or did he? And the Crier, Lorn? Were they keeping secrets, and if so, why? Such a devastat-ing thing should draw survivors closer together—to console and care for one another. But here, in one land, lived two completely isolated worlds. And they were at war with one another. Kai could not fathom this, and before he could begin to try he was knocked off balance again when the room came to a sudden stop. The door hissed open.

They walked out and then down a short, bright corridor to a door on the right, which opened as Lorn placed his fingertips on the raised square near its frame. Inside, there was a high-domed, large room that sloped away toward huge windows that were by far the most remarkable feature of the room. They rose from floor to ceiling and revealed the wide expanse of the cave through which he and Lorn had walked only moments before. For a brief instant, Kai felt as if he might slide down the slant of the floor and disappear out the window to fall hopelessly to the ground far below. He grabbed the back of the chair nearest him, then realized that they were not alone. Below, two people dressed in white, loose robes looked up at their entrance, smiling and patient.

Both women appeared young, attractive, friendly. As Lorn led him down the steps toward where they stood, Kai began to perceive them more clearly. They were middle-aged, only slightly younger than Lorn, but before he could form any other impressions, one raised her hand at their approach. "Welcome, brother. Don't be afraid. You won't fall out. I felt the same way when I first arrived."

"And so did I." The other offered her hand, too, and when Kai did not move to take either, they both moved closer themselves and touched him on his arms, looking directly into him as they did. It was there. Kai felt it with a twinge of nostalgia, like a sudden, unexpected image of home. They felt like him, and his face revealed it.

"Yes. But where are you from? Which village?" Kai blurted it out before he thought. This rashness caught him, flustered him into silence. They noticed this. He began to chastise himself for revealing too much.

"Please. Don't worry. Don't close up. You can't tell us anything we don't already know. There are no secrets here, only back there." Her voice trailed off. Had there been an edge, a flash of disgust, even hate at the end, or had Kai imagined it? "My name is Kare, and I come from the village to the west of yours. This is Lila, who came from the south. Perhaps, later, you can meet someone from your own village."

This cannot be, Kai's voice came to life to urge him to move cautiously. Can they still be here and not want to escape? And was she implying that he would be allowed after all to see his sisters? Or did they even know he was related to the girls stolen from his village?

"But it is a beautiful view from here, don't you think?" Kare had taken his elbow to move him toward the dizzying height beyond the window. As he looked down, he felt increasingly at ease, as if once more in his glider, free, above these things he did not understand.

Kare, studying him closely, seemed a bit puzzled. "You aren't afraid, I hope?" He smiled back at her. She looked to Lorn.

"I'm afraid we may need to specialize a program for our friend here. He came to us on the wind, so he knows what it is like to fly, something we've certainly lost, and he has already made some interesting connections. By the way, son, what is your name?"

He hesitated before he answered, but seeing no good to be gained from withholding or from fabricating a new name, he gave it. "Kai." Had there been the slightest raise of an eyebrow? If so, Lorn quickly recovered it.

"Well, Kai who can fly, we will dispense with the usual introduction to our world. You already know how things work, but I think you might find this interesting. Come. Sit down."

Before he moved back near Lorn, and after the two women had turned toward their own seats near him, Kai stretched out a tentative hand until it struck the cool, sturdy surface separating the outside from the in; he had sensed its presence in the lack of wind on his face, the complete absence of smells other than those near him. It was invisible, except for the slight distortion that came when he moved, the occasional fleeting reflection of light along its surface. Like every surface here, it was smooth and cool to the touch. His curiosity was not quite satisfied, but he turned back to Lorn and the women.

The seat was soft and comfortable, and gave way as he lowered his weight to it. As soon as they were all seated, the room became suddenly dark: thankfully, because later Kai realized that during the next moments his face revealed everything, yet because of that darkness his emotions had remained undetected. His mouth must have dropped open in his surprise and wonder. Later, his jaw ached, so he closed it, but at first there was no way to control his reactions to what he saw, so overpowering were the images before him and the mystery of their appearance.

The invisible surface over the windows grew darker, and then opaque. And as it grew dark it began to reveal a hazy outline that grew in definition proportionately to the gathering darkness. It began to lighten as Kai tried to determine what it was that was taking shape on the wall like some diffuse spirit rising from the mists. With a shudder, he recognized that it was a face. A huge face on which Kai could count the pores, if he had chosen, but he did not. The face was looking directly at him, towering in front of him like a commanding colossus and when he began to grow uneasy in his confusion and contemplated running from this inexplicable presence—this disembodied, unnatural face—her lips moved, and words tumbled into the darkness.

Her voice wrapped around him like a soothing garment. Its singsong ringing took him back, touched him deeply and removed the tension from the legs that were set to remove him from this place. But he did not listen to the words. They were insignificant compared to the overpowering being of the voice. It was the tone, the tone sweeping around him. The two did not fit together—sound and vision—and this was not right. She was not here; he could sense that. But where was she? Where was that body and face of natural proportions that produced this huge image? How, why is this happening? He wanted to look around, but could not find the nerve to move.

It was good that he did not, for the face suddenly vanished, as if sensing his uneasiness. It was replaced by a quickening series of images, one after another, bombarding him with flashes of people and places—images jumbled and incomprehensible. Some were vaguely familiar. There were the passageways, the short, white squat things that moved by themselves and hummed, and things he had never seen before that fulfilled he knew not what purpose. In each scene, however, there were people, people like him, laughing, playing, happy people. And children everywhere, running and laughing in and out of the foreground, their play having a strange effect on him, as if he had forgotten something very important. Throughout, the same calm, soft voice droned out of the darkness as the bright images dangled and danced in front of him: sunshine, greens, colorful robes and rooms. His mind could not encompass all the images. Each would take days to absorb and explore, and in his confusion, he began to open his ears to the words the voice spoke.

"The hard realities of life are so unnecessary. The drudgery of daily work that slowly grinds us down, gradually stoops and breaks us, does not exist here. We are happy in our ease. We are free from those forces that try to scar and maim us. Look at me." The voice's owner returned now, but she could be seen wholly, from head to toe. She wore a bright yellow dress that ended at mid-thigh, a fact that drew one's eyes to her legs. They were bare, long and shapely. She was shapely. The dress was tied at the waist, dipping low in front, and her arms were bare and soft above where they flexed at the elbows. Her hands stroked one another.

"How old am I?" She turned, and then smiled back over one shoulder. It was intended to attract, to challenge. Kai felt it clearly. She dared him to guess. If he looked at her and ignored the graying hair at her temples, he could guess her to be quite young, but he knew she was not. It was there, in the eyes above that haunting smile but nowhere else. Had she felt the touches of life? She would not tell them.

"I am old enough to be your great-grandmother, perhaps even your great-great-grandmother. Freedom from pain, cold, suffering, from the slavery of work and fear of sudden death means a long, and fulfilling life. More time to enjoy and explore." She talked as she walked off to her left as the foliage moved behind her. But this was only a momentary illusion that Kai was just beginning to compensate for when she came to rest beside a smoothly contoured pool. It had rocks and ferns on its farther edge and from them came the gurgle and splash of a small stream falling into the pool. In it sat a man, naked to the water line and smiling up at her. He was young, sleek and trim and unwrinkled. The woman dropped her robe to the floor. Kai did not have time to register his shock at seeing her naked. The young man's hand reached up to hers, and then there were only the two huge hands clasped in the darkness before him, slowly losing their definition and lapsing back into that total and impregnable darkness. Music rose softly from behind him. He enjoyed the sound and he wanted it to linger, but the light came back and Kai rose from his chair.

Kare smiled at him, and she perfectly glowed. Her eyes sparkled and she had again captured that image of youth and vitality, which he had felt when he first met her. He realized with a shock that he and Kare were alone. The others had withdrawn so quietly that he had not noticed, and the fact that they could do so made him immensely uncomfortable. She sensed this and came near him, covering with hers the hand he rested on the back of his chair. He looked down. Her hand glowed as well, and she brought her face close to his. Her breath, sweet and warm, rose and fell with her words.

"Don't be uneasy. We are here to help you grow. Now, come. You must be very hungry and food is ready. We'll eat, talk, relax. After a night's sleep, you'll feel much better, believe me."

Her voice lulled him, drew him along with it, and as he stiffened to walk beside her, he noticed that the opacity of the window covering had gone and through them he saw that it had grown dark outside. Twilight calmly descended and as he looked up, he could see the dim twinkling of the night lights above. Such an odd place. Such an odd and marvelous place, the voice within him murmured.

Chapter Seven
# Learning Woman

He woke slowly. In the luxury of the moment, he felt no compulsion to hurry. Instead, he stretched in the softness of the bed, a softness he had never known. He was so warm and content that he refused to open his eyes, but then the shock hit him. He was not in his own bed. The soft smoothness was only one clue. The lingering sweet scent on the covers over him was another, more powerful one. In the mild glow of mid-morning he remembered where he was; he recollected his so recent and vivid past.

His arm ached underneath its wrapping as he rolled over on his opposite side to look around. He was alone in the open, breezy and colorful room. The walls turned and disappeared in sharp angles. He was alone in the comfortable warmth of the bed and the memories of the night before. Only one night? Only one day here? Her tastes lingered on his tongue.

First, the foods, light and delicate and so sweet and juicy that he had doubted their existence, thought them merely a tasteful illusion. He had never eaten anything remotely similar, and as Kare coaxed him to try another, and then another, and as he grew fat, content, and sleepy, she drew closer, then closer, until she warmed his side with her glow. He looked at her, as if from a distance watching them both, and realized that he had never been so close to a woman who was not also a relative. But he was lazy, curious, wallowing in a tepid, welcomed fog. Her outlines grew hazy and indistinct, and then he felt her on his lips.

Her mouth was soft and tasted of the juices of their dinner. As he moved with her, he realized that he liked this touching that sent a shiver down his spine, then throughout his body. It was if he were awakening, this touching was so intense. Her face went away, only to look down on his as he reclined against the cushion behind him. He grew confused, and as he began to come around to address this new confusion, she withdrew again, this time rising, drawing him with her.

Hand in hand, she led him around one of the many corners in the room to a pool. It was not like the other, exactly, not like the one with the falling water and young man, but it was warm and scented, and it made him relax again once he could slip below its smooth and giving surface and find solitude under the water for his growing embarrassment. She had taken his clothes off for their swim, and he had never been naked in front of a woman before. Still below the surface, he swam, finding a submerged bench along the far edge, and as he slipped up on it he looked back at Kare.

She stood naked on the edge of the pool and, without causing a ripple, she dove into the water and came to him underneath. His confusion mounted. He looked away as the distance between them narrowed, but he did not want to. Although his mind was suddenly awake and racing, he could not unravel the mounting, flashing images that demanded his attention. He tried to think of other things (his family, his friends, the long lighted corridors outside) but each seemed to return him automatically and logically to this pool, to this smiling woman.

Yes. Kai could remember every minute detail: the smell of the water, the play of the light upon the ripples they made. Every detail and the feelings came back in a rush so powerful that he grew wider awake thinking of it again.

He looked around the room. It was sparsely furnished and decorated in light colors such as he had never seen before he came here. On the low table beside the bed he saw garments. Rising into the warm air of the morning, he examined them. They were like Lorn's, but tighter, and since his own clothes were not to be found near the pool or where they had eaten, he returned to the table and picked them up. They must be meant for him, but before beginning the arduous task of putting them on, he returned to the pool.

He was surprised to find the water still warm. After soaking for a while on the submerged bench, he removed the coverings on his wounds. They had become saturated the night before. The smaller one on his side had come off in their bed so he decided to remove the one on his arm as well. To his utter amazement, the wound had almost healed. Although there was still some redness and puffiness under the skin, the surface itself had smoothed and shrunken until only a short white scar remained. These people must have powerful healers, he thought. Perhaps I can learn their secrets, take them home for the people.

He thought of his father and suddenly felt very close to

him, wishing that he were here to help explain these strange happenings, this equally odd sensation when Kare kissed him. With such powerful medicine, perhaps his father would have been saved, and his mother, who was even now dying slowly. His sisters. He rose from the pool, refreshed.

He dried as Kare had shown him, with a piece of a fabric kept for that purpose, and returned to the clothes near the bed. However, as he held them, first this way then that, to better survey the various slits and holes, he felt a presence behind him. Guessing that Kare had returned, in his excitement he turned to meet her.

Her smile wavered, but only briefly, as she scanned his nakedness quickly and thoroughly, before moving to her left to cover his befuddlement as he moved to cover himself with the foreign, alien and unaccommodating garments. She came close, to help, and her nearness calmed him, oddly enough. "I am sorry. I thought you were someone else." She did not respond, but simply began to help him sort out what went where.

"I know. Kare. I heard about this only this morning from my father. In fact, we had quite a discussion about this type of modified 'orientation'."

He stopped dead still. Of course. It had all been planned, but to hear it come so matter-of-factly from someone else made his backbone stiffen. He was being manipulated, drawn along, and his face became hard and unforgiving. He jerked the shirt from her hands and pulled it roughly over his head himself.

"Don't get angry at me! This was not my doing. And things have been straightened out. Kare has been sent on a trip, to keep her busy elsewhere. I will help you adjust, personally."

But this was not what she had intended to say, nor the way she had intended to say it. This boy flustered her, tangled her thoughts and threw them against her emotions. But she was also still angry, and this had put an unwanted edge to her voice. It had even more of an edge when she had heard about Lorn's decision to alter the orientation for this one, to experiment on him for some unknown reason. Her anger had been immediate, clear, profound, and after he had smiled momentarily in an "I thought so" smile, he wilted under that anger.

Now, she would see to things herself, and she would be completely open and honest, as this young man deserved, if she could get him to return that openness now that his pride had been hurt and his anger had taken him over. He felt used, toyed with, and she could not blame him, but men—she well knew—were such fragile beings.

"I am truly sorry. Believe me. There is no excuse, although father keeps blaming it on you. You were a surprise. He had to compensate, and all that. But that is no reason, for, for . . ." Her eyes swept to the bed, and the image of his naked back, smooth and contoured to his thighs, and then, when he had turned . . . "for these methods. We should get going."

"I'm not going anywhere, unless it's out of this place." To accentuate his pronouncement, he sat on the table.

"Look. I understand your anger. I said I'm sorry. I promise that I'll be honest with you. I will help you understand. Believe me. No lies. No deception. I don't know if you've been told, but no one stays here against her will. After the orientation and cooling down period, you are free to go.

Nobody ever does."

"Cooling down period?"

"All we want is the chance to show you who we are, what we do, how we live. Then, we want you to think about it rationally, logically, objectively. That's how decisions are made, and people decide to stay."

He looked at her closely. She believed every word, every implied truth behind the words, and her conviction shined on her face. He would see how far that conviction led, how far her promise would carry her. "I will wait. I will see, as long as I have time."

She took this as agreement and joy crept slowly over her. "Good. Now let's go eat. I don't know about you, but I'm starved."

He was, indeed, hungry.

From this easy decision in the morning, to the difficult one that evening, the day became a blur for Kai. A simple thing like breakfast became a nightmare of bewilderment, inadequate explanations and compacted images. They ate in a large room with many other people grouped about the tables that filled it. Some of them looked at him out of the corners of their eyes, others over their shoulders as they talked with their companions, and this made him self-conscious and therefore uncomfortable.

Then, there was the food. It was tasty, and there was a lot of it, but there were no fires—the lack of which, oddly, he had somehow anticipated—but also no people preparing it—which he had not. Instead, he and Ursla drew what they wanted from holes in the wall, yet the food came out hot and steaming. She tried to explain it as they ate, but her words were strangers to him and he did not understand, so to hide his ignorance, he simply nodded and saved the impressions for later.

This technique he employed all day long as they went from room to room, from corridor to corridor. She showed him huge whining objects and he sensed the ominous power they possessed, but could not decipher their purpose or how they were made, despite her long talk about them. There was the place where babies were born, this had been easy and encouraging, but when she spoke of this, she became abrupt and hurriedly talked about baby rules. It was all confusing, and only two points from the whole day remained strong in his memory.

The first was a room, dark and close. In it, several people sat with their eyes trained before them on row after row of lighted images, bright windows. There was movement in some of them, none in others, but as Ursla talked he heard and understood the significance of what his eyes confirmed. The images were of the mountainside—its ridges and canyons, trails and forests. And in one, the raiding party was shown climbing a steep trail on a treeless slope. He could see his sisters in the middle of the group, but he stifled his reactions, pretending to look about him, but fully intent upon this one, clear image. He asked how these pictures came to be, using the time it took to answer to examine the image more closely. They had not traveled far in two days. Why? Had the people come, only to be slaughtered again? Yet the raiders' numbers did not seem to be diminished.

She noted his attention. "They are inside. That was yesterday. They will be here, with us, in a day or two." She read his other thought. "No. They have not come. See for yourself." She pointed to a wide expanse of mountain clearing. It was calm, serene, undisturbed in its greenery. Then she indicated a trail. It was deserted. "I can't tell you how glad we are. That's our farthest camera, and no one has come up the trail. Perhaps reason has taught them the futility. I hope so."

She moved him to the back of the room, then around and back to the door. Although he understood little of what she said, he noted every detail of what he saw: the number of men, their placement.

The other clear impression, out of the press and clutter of a day of confusion, came while they rested in the grass below the bright sun. They had been on the brittle grass only a short time before she said what had obviously been on her mind a long while.

"Your people. Why did they keep coming to attack us, time after time? Why do they keep fighting us?" His look of incredulity, his raised eyebrows did nothing more than spur her to a more emphatic demand. "Well, why?"

"That is an odd question, from a people who attack us, time after time. Who raid our villages, leave them burning and people hurt or dead as they drag our people off, never to be seen again." He had allowed too much emotion to creep into his voice. They must not know that he had a very special, a very personal interest in them and in their captives. For some reason, he felt it better to hide his relation to the new captives. If they knew, they could use his sisters against him, hide them away so that he could not get to them, but there was something else.

"I know, it seems cruel and brutal, but it's absolutely necessary, crucial, as you'll see. But I meant, why do they keep dying, sacrificing themselves by choice in such a hopeless attempt to save others?"

The look of disbelief on his face stopped her cold. She felt his question first, and then his understanding. It was her turn to feel ignorant and backward. "We do it, because we care for one another. If we did not, we would not be who we are. We are humans."

She blushed slightly, and turned away to scan the buildings in the Center. So odd. Such a simple reason, such a simple people. But it compelled them to the thoughtless sacrifice of the most important thing in the whole universe: one's self. To endure pain, to anticipate such a loss, and to do it for another. Such a primitive bond was so difficult to grasp, and so obviously counterproductive. How could anything ever be accomplished, how could their society ever progress, if they spent all their time worrying about the others, those who may get hurt? She turned her gaze back to him. He was watching three children play. Their guardian sat on a bench watching them, too. His attention turned to Kai, but then he recognized Ursla and quickly turned back to his charges.

Could Kai have such self-less dedication to a mate? She knew they were monogamous, newcomers had told her that, but she had found it a difficult concept to understand. To have only one man to desire, and then possess only that one, seemed somehow unnatural, somehow unhealthy. But it intrigued her, as did their obvious willingness to die for one another. This intensity, this power seemed almost holy, a sacred fanaticism that she wanted to explore, perhaps use, and this boy could be the key, if she could get him to open up to her. Damn that Kare, she thought. She would pay.

"I answered your question, now you answer mine?"

She recovered quickly. "I'll try."

He remained quiet for a moment longer, trying to phrase it the way he had thought it, so that there could be no way to turn it aside. "You said you had to raid our villages. You said it was necessary. Why?"

Her father had warned her, as he left her to her own decision that very morning, and now she began to understand his reservations. This boy did strike to the heart of matters. He possessed an intellect she had not expected. Most of his people were overwhelmed into silence here. They grew taciturn, introspective, and then, one day as the obvious ease of the lifestyle here became equally overwhelming, they accepted. It was simple. It had been done numerous times and a pattern had emerged that nurtured this process of adaptation, but now . . .. He asked too many questions, and forgot too little. True, they were logical questions, and at times even obvious, but in the past, they were never asked at all. This was the challenge. She would see how far his intellect would reach. "To put it bluntly, we need new genes, and we need uncontaminated breeders."

It was too blunt, and once again the language failed him, with one exception: breeders. "You take our people as mates?" In his mouth, it sounded as odd and illogical as it appeared in his mind, but somehow it began to make sense to Kai. This could explain why no one ever returned. One does not leave one's family. "It is an odd form of courtship. Did you ever think of coming as friends, and not as enemies?"

It was her turn to be surprised. "Of course, I keep forgetting. Your priests keep you in the dark. They use their mumbo-jumbo to frighten you, and use us as the evil force that keeps you afraid. With that type of fear, what reception would we get?" But she did not want to pursue this line too soon, prematurely. He would be offended. He would close up and this would not do. He needed history, but only at the right time and certainly not now, before his trust had been gained. She thought to direct him away.

"Anyway, our people are ill. There's a sickness here that we can't defeat. We can't even understand it. Somehow, it's deep within us, and when we mate with our own, it becomes more widespread, more powerful. Even our children sometimes get it. We've tried everything, but we aren't as good at this as we used to be. Too much of the old knowledge was lost." And this, too, came too close for now, but she could see that she had touched something in him, some pocket of sympathy perhaps. "It's a terrible illness. It wastes people to shells, before death takes them." She noted his agitation.

"But we have that, too. It killed my father; it is killing my mother." He saw it. Although her face remained frozen, she was straining to maintain her composure. Then, there was the imprint of resolve in her features. She was, indeed, a powerful woman, and again he felt close to her and she felt familiar.

"Come. We need to have the doctor check your wounds. Do they hurt? How did you get them?" Although she knew he would not tell her, she asked anyway to keep him focused away from the direction their talk had taken. She did not need an answer. A laser burn was unmistakable, and they had fired at him several times. But there was also the one rear guard who had not returned to meet up with the party. Could he be responsible for her absence? This was one aspect she wished to understand, this brutality so oddly balanced against his dedication to life. It was an odd paradox indeed. So, she chattered their way to the clinic and ordered the tests.

After an afternoon of being poked and prodded, Kai found himself watching the evening from the top of one of the tall houses in the Center. It was open, and there were shrubs, trees, grass, and even a pool on top. In the twilight, he could sense the nearness of the night lights as they popped into being, but his eyes tricked him into believing that they were far away. Like everything else here, they were illusion, a sham, and he was ready to leave, soon.

He needed only a few more pieces to the puzzle, a few more scraps of information to find his way: the way to his sisters, the way to disable the room they watched the mountainside from, a way to weapons. These thoughts were on his mind as she came up behind him, and she felt them surge and well up inside him, like hot, molten rock.

"How can you do it? Kill like that?"

Although her question lacked specificity, it worked his memory as surely as if a button had been pushed: the arrow through the opening and the raider's eyes, the rocks rolling down upon the three, the upturned gaze of wonderment on the one behind. And with the memories came the revulsion as clearly and strongly as it had come before, first, and then later, every time he found time to let his thoughts drift uncontrolled. The urge to double over and retch crept over him like death itself, like the spirit of death itself, and she felt this too.

She turned him with a slight pressure on his elbow and the grief and despair on his young face told the story, and her estimation of him grew proportionately. He was not the savage she had imagined when the report had arrived and the guards set out to capture him. "What happened?"

Her concern was earnest and heartfelt. It struck him deeply and, losing his reserve, he told her all: the fire, the wound, the arrow, the intense flash. His voice was strong, it did not quaver, but, then, it did not hide the seed of guilt, either.

She took his arm again, after he had fallen silent, and led him to a green, cushioned couch near the pool and waterfall. "You mustn't be too harsh on yourself. All the people who go out know that they may not return. Most of them, in fact, hope they will not. All of them have the disease, you see, and their futures are not bright. Here, they will waste away in front of the others, become weak and powerless, as they die slowly. Outside there is a chance to go quickly as they help to bring in their replacements and the new genes. It's quite noble, don't you think?"

The eyes above the arrow came back to him. They were hollow, sunken, and he recognized that look of hopelessness. He had watched it grow in his father.

"She did what she had to do: destroy herself and her weapon. You didn't kill her, actually. She did it herself, as was right."

"She?"

"Vivian. She led the raid in. Another had command of the withdrawal. So, she volunteered for the rear guard. It was just like her. It was her choice, and a good one."

"I killed a woman?"

"She would have killed you, if she could have. Fortunately, she didn't."

"But why a woman?" His voice was no longer as steady as before.

Ursla noted this with a great deal of curiosity, but with the curiosity came a quandary that made her speech halting, her thoughts erratic. It was as if he, trying to speak the gibberish of another language, had revealed how truly and vastly different they were. "Although we allow a few men to go, periodically, on an outside excursion, the raiding parties are always comprised solely of women. This is only right. It is their responsibility."

It was his turn to show his confusion as in the growing silence he looked about him, seeing nothing. But he could go only so far, and then there were the barriers again, so he stopped trying and let his mind return, shorn of any need to do other than see and feel in the moment. There was something vaguely familiar about this place. He had not realized it before, when their talk was what demanded his attention. He felt suddenly as if he had been here before, and then she seemed also so familiar. The small waterfall gurgled beside him.

They sat in silence as the darkness descended around them. Just as it seemed endless, this calm and serene setting was disturbed by a short peel of light music coming from inside. As Ursla rose, colored lights appeared in the pool, which Kai had been staring at so long he had forgotten why. She disappeared through the door and lights sprang on to mark her passage through her house. He felt no need to stir, so he fell back to regarding the pool. Such a strange place. Wonderful, but so only because it was new and different and required examination, understanding. If the wonder remains afterward, he thought, perhaps this is a good thing after all. It is easy, easy, easy. Then he wondered what it was worth.

His thoughts were interrupted by hasty, muffled voices from within. He could not make out what they were saying, only individual, vague words. Rising from the couch he moved around the pool and to the far side of the terrace near the door. As he came closer, he recognized Lorn's voice, and that he was angry, at least his voice had that edge to it and he spoke too quickly with a suppressed, intense volume. His heat and eagerness were equally answered with cool reserve.

"I apologized for that, but it was Kare's idea and I think it might have worked, given time, but this . . .this . . . you of all people should not be involved. He's trouble. Since he's been here, he's been nothing but a disruptive force. He's a savage. He's cruel and heartless and dangerous, and you've taken him into secure zones. He is not ready, and may never be, for that. You don't even have your guard."

She waited until his energy failed him, and responded slowly, subdued yet deliberate. "He poses no threat. Quite the contrary. Properly educated, he may be of great benefit to us. And I decide what I should or should not get involved in. I will remind you that I am no longer your child." The silence she left to underscore the fact would not be endured.

"What do you mean, properly educated? I know you. You go too far. You're too self-centered, always looking to press the limits. You'll reveal too much!"

"Thank you for your opinion, father. It has been noted. Now, good night."

"If you give away too much you'll regret it. The Council . . ."

"Lorn. Good night."

And then there was only the intensity of the silence. Kai moved back to the pool where he slipped quickly out of his clothes and dove toward the bottom. He was surprised to find it so deep and as he rose to the surface he caught a blurred image above him. He gasped as he broke the surface, and then did a quick backstroke to the far side where a bench just below the surface acted as a step as well as a seat as in Kare's pool. He rested on this, the water lapping his chest. Remaining completely quiet, he smiled his challenge.

She glanced at the pile of his clothes at her feet and accepted without hesitation. Her fluid plunge into the depths was a thing of beauty, marking her frequent use of the pool. It was a vision, a dream, and then she was seated next to him, breathing in short gasps. The water gleamed with the light from below as she gave him a shy, sincere smile. The water had dissolved her reserve, making her fresh and open.

He had so many more questions as they sat there, ones springing of their own accord and volition from the feeling he had for her at that one moment. But he could not find the words; they seemed suddenly irrelevant and inconsequential. Kai began to swim—at first hesitant and self-conscious—and then he dove into a playful game of tag and catch that Ursla, first grudgingly, joined until each grew exhausted. As they sat once more on the bench, breathless and uplifted, the small waves of their play caressed them. Kai felt relaxed and contented. Each fleeting thought came wrapped in its own warm glow, curiously requiring only recognition, and no action whatsoever. Things seemed clearer now.

"I've seen this pool before." She raised one eyebrow, and then slowly lowered it.

"Ah, yes. The show. That was Shiela, the first director. The orientation was her idea, and it worked, all along, till now." She grew pensive, reflective in her silence.

"Why is it different now?"

She shook herself awake, and returned. "Because your people have the disease, which should not have happened, since contact between our peoples has been restricted to those who we bring inside and then closely monitor. The raiding parties are specially equipped, to eliminate the potential for contamination of your villages." She grew silent once more. "But also because your people have begun to change as a result of the raids. Your presence demonstrates that. No one else before made it as far. And now, your people don't attack. Why? Are they planning? Frightened? Developing their strategies? All I know for sure is that they are changing, and we are not."

He mulled this over. He had not considered himself as a representative of change, or of his people, but this woman beside him seemed to. Perhaps it was true. Perhaps his people were changing. He was young, so he had not seen much of what was before, but the old people were always saying that things were different today. The villages are larger, the game less abundant, the days warmer and drier, and the children less respectful, less concerned. He had acted out of selfishness when he left the village to save his sisters, and he had disobeyed or ignored the traditions of leadership and service, so perhaps it was true, perhaps things were changing. He wondered if this could be good, or bad.

He bit off the impulse to share these ideas with her, to tell her of Luther and his stories and vision of the past he had been given in the fire by the old man. He also swallowed the impulse to tell her how the villagers talked of the raiders, the vague stories and murmurings that frightened children and that might make her reconsider and argue for the raids to continue as before. Instead of telling her his thoughts, he phrased a question.

"Today, you said the raids were necessary, because of the disease, but you didn't say why the raids and not some other way, in the beginning. Why couldn't your people simply come to mine and ask for help when the disease first came? Lorn told me that, in the past, we were kin. We help our kin. We do not kill them, or turn away from them when they need us."

She studied him for a long time. The water grew chilled, or perhaps it was simply her. To hold off the need to answer, to gain time to decide how much to tell, she rose up out of the pool and walked around it to her robe. It felt wonderfully warm as she picked it up and straightened it out to be put on. Not to be put off, Kai had followed her, and now wrestled with his own, unfamiliar clothes. When they were once more on the soft couch, she leaned against him, her face toward the lights twinkling above their rooftop perch, and began.

"My father told you the truth. Long ago, your people and mine lived together, here, in this city. There weren't as many of us, so there was plenty of room, but as families grew and as people began to live longer, it became cramped. Some moved outside, there, onto the shoulders of the mountains and the plains beyond, even on the far side of the mountains from where your people live today. But the people outside became increasingly hostile toward my people. They accused us of things, made threats against us, called us vile names. Finally, they started to have an effect on our people here, drawing some away from us with lies, loud demands, strange ideas." She took several deep breaths before she continued the recitation.

"Then, the words turned to actions. Some inside who were lured by the ideas of the outside fanatics turned traitor. They struck in the night, wrecking important machinery, destroying crucial files, smashing labs, and then escaped outside where their allies waited. My people chased after, because the traitors had not only ruined our home but also carried off some of our most valued treasures: books, records, knowledge. We had to have them back, you see. But when we came out onto the plains below, they were waiting. My people were slaughtered. Only a few survived to return with their stories, leaving the dead and wounded, and our things behind. That is the type of treatment we received from your people, and that is why we live here, with our defenses to protect us, and go out only when we need to. How could you expect us to come to ask for help?"

His eyes were wide with wonder, so she put it to rest with a brief and abrupt epilogue. "Unfortunately, our treasures were never found. They were destroyed in the fighting, or else by those who betrayed us, because we returned to try to recapture them. Better prepared this time, we came away with a great victory, but in the fighting the land was laid waste, your people scattered."

He was once more dumbfounded. Each new revelation in this odd and disturbing place brought new frustrations. So this is how it began? At least, this is how she believes it began. He sensed the sincerity behind her words. She believed, for as she spoke her indignation and temperature had risen. She believes the words, right or wrong.

He was learning, and now he understood that in the most profound deception lay a seed of truth. Her story would explain a great deal, perhaps even his own people's ignorance. Or were they ignorant of this past, this kinship gone terribly wrong? He wished the Crier were still alive and he needed to speak with Luther. He needed to stop the attack, if he could. They needed to reconsider, but for the moment, he must put Ursla at ease while he gathered more information.

"I'm beginning to see. But all this was a long time ago. They were other people, not us. I think we could understand one another. We could work together. My people don't know you, except as killers and kidnappers. They think you may not even be human beings. If they knew, they wouldn't be afraid. I'm sure of it." A ray of possibility came to life. It showed on her face, and this reaction did not go unnoticed, or unappreciated, nor did he miss the bleak reaction to his next words.

"I need to speak with them, to explain." Her frown cut him off cold.

"That would be extremely difficult, perhaps impossible." But the potential for reconciliation obviously intrigued her. She was weighing the benefits against the possible dangers. If it were controlled carefully in the early stages, and if they could withdraw quickly enough if things went badly . . .

His disappointment weighed heavily upon her. "I'll try, but even my orders can be countermanded by our Council. We'll see."

His brows furrowed and this questioning look caught her attention. Didn't he believe that she was sincere, that she would do as she said and work for a meeting between the two peoples? That she would desire understanding and co-operation above violence, raids, death? She felt hurt and misunderstood. "You don't believe that I will try?"

"Who are you?"

The sting turned to anger. Could he think her so small, so non-consequential that he could dismiss her so easily? Despite the Council, she could do a lot, and now this dull savage called her a no one.

"What do you mean?" Her heat rose.

"I mean, who are you here. In this place." The sweep of his hands took in a full circuit of the city, and the truly honest, benign look on his face dulled her anger. But then the anger was replaced by disbelief. Perhaps he had not been told, and despite his intelligence he had not guessed. She melted for him.

"Kai, I'm the Director."

Chapter Eight
# Turning Tales

They spent a long time together that night, and in their talk and his silences she searched for signs that his idea of her had changed, that he saw her differently. But, unless she was wholly mistaken, and she never was, he did not. He was unimpressed by their power structure. Given the past villagers' reports of the oddities in their primitive society, this made sense. As a woman, she probably didn't count for much in his scheme of things. And yet, when she tried to explain their hierarchy, he was interested, even prodded her to elaborate. Perhaps he could be taught. After all she had learned from him, as the two exchanged details of their lives and the ways of their people. She had eagerly answered each of his interruptions and listened to him tell of his village. The possibility of any other social order had never captured her imagination, as it did now, here in the dark with Kai speaking so warmly near her.

That women could make decisions and direct the people had never occurred to him. She could tell that he understood the concept and that he could understand the implications as she explained this way of her people to him. He felt it, too, the logic of it, but she needed to handle this lesson very carefully as she talked. If he could accept it, he might stay and their troubles could be resolved. This was new territory for her. He was the first outside male in a long time so it made sense that his orientation might require different methods. Where it would all lead, she had no clue. His questions had been simple, straightforward: "But why? How?"

"Why not?" Her answer stopped him, as did the facts. Of all the people, few possessed the equally acute evolutions of intellect and intuition, of reason and instinct. For these few, there was no difference between ways of knowing. In any crisis for a group of people, only a few could decide, quickly and accurately, based upon both insight and logic, and these few were women.

Although she at first hesitated, she decided to press further, cursing herself for doing so in case this proved to be a problem later. At the moment, it seemed right and appropriate for him to know. "The woman you saw in the show, with Kare and Lorn, Shiela? She was the first Director, the one who changed things. She recognized your people's power. We had been so long to ourselves that we lost something—the power to imagine, perhaps, or the power to go beyond the confines of reason and logic.

She recognized that intuition and insight are limited to what we know and experience. We were locked inside this mountain for our own safety, so we did not think outside. Call it what you will. Our ancestors have called it many things. The fact remained. Your people had something we lacked at a time when we needed it desperately. So, the raids began because she saw that the disease was related to this lack, somehow. We couldn't understand this illness in the ways we understood everything else, so we needed something new." She could sense that he was trying to imagine the steps that would have taken the Director to that decision without first considering the obvious step of calling for help.

"She selected young women from the villages. She showed them how we live and they stayed. They lived well, had a say in things, and had babies. That was seven generations ago, and I am one of their descendants. Now, I am the Director."

There had been no challenge to her decision. It was a logical move, especially once the effects were seen. Healthy babies, friendly and contented newcomers. And the decisions. Although there was actually very little to direct on a daily basis—when life wore on at a machine's pace from day to day with one day pretty much like another, and the systems worked so well that they required no alteration—there still appeared, at times, a major dilemma. Then, a choice was required, and the Director made it, based upon reason, logic and, in Ursla's case, a new insight heightened by new blood. Others were glad not to have to make such important decisions, that is until recently. This conflict with Lorn was touchy, indeed, but she did not feel compelled to raise this exception to her rule.

Then, when Kai's agitation showed he wanted to pursue this further, she cut the explanations short with a brushing kiss by way of leave-taking before they went to sleep. It would not do to reveal all, to unravel things too far, and he had been on the point of taking them back to origins, and this would not do. Directors knew the secrets of origins. They knew how the world came into being. And only they knew.

That is, unless some of his people knew as well. And if they did, perhaps something remained from that time of battle and rebellion—some old animosity, or (she dared not hope) some scrap of something else more important. She would need to direct things cautiously, and in the night she struck a compromise. Contact would be made with his people, but not by him. One of the new captives even now going through orientation so well would return to her people, when she was prepared.

The next morning at a hastily called meeting of the Council she shared her idea and it accepted her plan, but not without dissent. Lorn was loud and outspoken against it, and he had swayed several men and a councilwoman to his side. He argued for continued isolation, using Kai's murder of the raiders and, ironically, the disease to justify his case.

This conflict, however, did not trouble her as much as the one she had with Kai. The compromise did not sit well with him. She saw it in his eyes and felt it in his stiffened composure when she touched him. To put him at ease, she offered to let him go with her to speak with the new captives, and to decide which one would go to his people. There were two, but only one could go. She intended to interview them both and then decide which should receive the intense, shortened orientation that would train her quickly as their emissary. He could prove useful in the choice, either knowingly or unwittingly. At least the offer seemed to calm him, and he turned his interests back, once more, to her and to learning more about this world.

But Kai had two minds. With one he imagined a life here, with Ursla. He enjoyed her company, her touch. And, the benefits of this easy life were apparent everywhere he looked. However, his compulsion toward his people was strong, pulling him on and demanding that he look for the means to rejoin them, with both his sisters. He imagined several complex and dramatic plans, but found instead the simplest device of all.

On each of his excursions, he had charted the intricate hallways as best he could in his head. It was an easy plan to remember, once he looked past the bright lights and hurrying crush of people. He only needed to deal with a small segment of the huge network. There were two main halls: the largest and most often used was immediately before the gigantic cave, running parallel to its long course; the other was shorter and perpendicular to the first, moving away from the Center. In it was the room where they watched the mountainside, and Kai assumed that this hallway was dedicated to defense.

And if it was there to defend, he thought, it would lay between threat and heart. The outside had to be connected to this hall. The weapons and his sisters were somewhere along its course, perhaps on one of its shorter, tributary halls. Then, as he pondered the probability of success if he were to steal weapons, disable the surveillance room, find his sisters, and fight his way to the outside, he stumbled quite by accident across an alternative.

While he thought through this thing on their way back to the eating room, he felt the pressing urge to pee. He slowed, but then, since they were in the middle of the outer hallway and there were no bushes near, he tried to appear untroubled by his need as he asked her where. She led him a short distance to a door on their left and pointed to it, remaining behind as he went towards it. As he neared it, the door hissed open and a man came out—glanced quickly at Kai, then Ursla—and turned down the corridor. Kai stepped inside.

The interior was not so different from the other rooms he had visited, white and non-personal. He stepped to one wall, under which a trench ran, where he relieved himself. The air was close in the small room so he hurried and as he was adjusting his clothes he looked to the door. He had considered it before: these doors and he did not get along well.

He tried his hand on the raised square. Nothing. He tried again, this time touching only his fingertips as he had seen others do. Nothing. He tried again and again, with identical lack of results. He was trapped. Barring any fortunate entrance by someone, he was trapped in this close room and a deep ancient fear grabbed him. He began to pound on the door with his fists, evenly at first but then more forcefully, not out of panic but with urgency. Ursla came to his rescue.

She found his dilemma humorous and teased him a bit, but then she saw his claustrophobia draped about him like a shawl. He would not admit it, but it was there in his darkened eyes, so she took him back toward the outside hallway and to an intersecting passage with the bright colors that he had come to recognize as a warning. She turned right, into new territory, and stopped at one of the first doorways. As it opened, Kai was taken by the red sign on its door: a jagged bolt of lightening.

Inside, there was the high pitched scream he had heard in muffled, subdued tones throughout his stay, but had grown almost accustomed to since his first fearful day. Here, it was louder, more distinct and insistent. To one side of the darkened room there was a well-lighted alcove, and once they stepped into its bright recess, the noise all but disappeared.

A man sat at a table, oblivious to their arrival until Ursla's voice startled him awake. Kai did not understand what she said, but when she nodded toward the man, who had risen and walked back out into the larger room, he understood that he was to follow.

In a far corner, they stepped into yet another quiet alcove. The lights came on as the man took Kai's right hand. He resisted at first, but as he looked into the man's eyes he could sense his lack of concern over what for him must have been a common ritual, but also, below that, a mounting fear, as yet undefined or recognized. Kai realized that it was he who made this man fearful, so he relaxed and allowed his hand to be placed on a cold, metal surface, where it was held flat, fingers spread out like a leaf. A bright light flashed and rolled below it from left to right, and back again. He could feel its warmth, and then all was dark again.

"Easy enough. Right?" Kai nodded. "Say, you're the savage, aren't you?" He nodded again, this time more slowly and less friendly as he tried to hide his growing hardness whenever that term was thoughtlessly used. "I've heard about you." Kai forced a smile, then returned to Ursla, who thanked the man in a perfunctory way as they left.

"What was all that for?"

"I forgot that your prints had not been placed on file. No wonder you couldn't open doors."

Mulling this over, he turned right as they entered the hallway, but she quickly caught his elbow and gently but firmly turned him back the way they had come. "What was all that in the room?"

She slid around the question too easily, too hastily again, and he noted this, too. He phrased his next carefully, but put it aside. He would need to ask it later, in the right context, after some time had elapsed to obscure its connection to this moment, and this place.

He asked it over lunch in the noise of the dining hall. As they finished their small meal, he asked if there was another men's room nearby. She pointed to it. He did not take long, just long enough, and when he returned to the table he chuckled. "I can't go into one of those without laughing about what happened this morning. To tell the truth, I was beginning to get a bit scared when you came to my rescue. I didn't know how I was going to get out. Don't you ever worry—about getting trapped in a room?" He tried to keep his voice steady and believable and to appear truly concerned, even a bit frightened.

"Don't worry. They're foolproof. If one fails, you can always call for help. There are communicators in almost every room. Besides, you can force open the doors. It's hard, but possible. Don't worry, though. It never happens. You're safe."

≈

That evening Kai asked about the visit with the captives she had mentioned. He did not press hard, but when she stiffened, he either turned to a new subject or rationalized his request, simply. "It is a matter of importance, for both our peoples, that we make contact soon. Wouldn't it be best to do it now, to get your process started in case they are still going to attack?"

Reluctantly, she agreed, and since he dropped so easily back to talk of insignificant and unrelated things, she believed him sincere and brought the subject up again later, herself. "I guess it doesn't matter. The women should be through with today's orientation activities. They're probably relaxing. We might as well join them. Perhaps you can help put them more at ease."

A short while later, Kai felt his frustration return. Since his first encounter with this new world, he had been impressed, almost overwhelmed by its size, its obviously monstrous proportions, its ceaseless motion, its power. But, he was also beginning to think that, like everything else here, this may be an illusion. Ursla's people went nowhere. They hid in their hole and remained the same.

Their hole was made up on illusions, too; even distance was a trick upon the eye, the mind. He had imagined his sisters far away, somewhere far away behind guards and massive doors, locked away to protect them from him. This, of course, was an image of his own construction. It came from people's reaction when they saw him and the fear he seemed to generate in them.

They did not want to engage him, so he imagined they would do anything to keep him under control and the image of security and size had grown proportionately, becoming so strong that it had directed everything he had done—almost everything—and now, when this image was shattered suddenly, he was left stunned, his sense of proportion shaken, and his youthful exuberance in his ability to frighten people with his presence popped like a bubble. However, the moment also rejuvenated his confidence in his ability to overcome adversity. His voice returned after its long nap.

To get to his sisters, they simply returned to the room they had visited that morning. Ursla stepped through the door with the lightening bolt on it after telling him to wait in the corridor. She returned immediately and they continued down the hallway toward its darkened end. Here, there was a door. A simple door, slightly larger but nonetheless identical to every one he had seen. She touched the raised square, and the door hissed open onto another, shorter passage.

As they moved down it, though, he noticed large windows on his left. He had not considered this possibility. Nevertheless, he stroked the cool, invisible coverings, and breathed deeply as he imagined the feel of the cold wind of twilight beyond. They revealed the mountainside below, and he suddenly realized that this was real, not an illusion. His hopes rose. As they walked he counted the windows.

His sisters were in a room halfway down the corridor across from the third window. As the door opened to Ursla's touch, Kai caught a flicker of surprise on those within. There were three older women, relaxed and reclining on low couches. One was familiar; she had been in the room with Kare when they first met. And there were his sisters, dressed identically to the older women, and equally relaxed. There were also three men, standing close to their respective walls, silently waiting.

His sisters did not attempt to hide their surprise. "Kai!"

Lori, the smallest, was on her feet immediately, before she could catch his warning look. Nata remained seated, while Ursla surveyed the scene carefully. As Lori and he exchanged a brief hug, he smiled back at her. "We grew up together in the village. I know her family." His hurried explanation seemed to console Ursla, since it corresponded with the reports, so she moved closer to Lilian and beckoned her aside, perhaps to explain the unusual visit.

Smiling all the while and doing his best to appear calm and at ease, Kai maneuvered Lori back to Nata's chair. "Don't give us away. Get ready. When I leave the room, work your way toward the door. Wait there." With brief spurts, he outlined his simple plan, dictating their parts in it. He did not have much time before Ursla returned and called for drinks. The men went out, only to return immediately with trays crowded with cups. As they gathered around the central table, Kai whispered into Ursla's ear and she smiled.

"Two doors down." He left the room quietly.

First, he opened the door to the men's room to make sure there was no attendant inside. Then, he ran back up the hallway toward the corridor's end, exploring quickly. Coming to a corner, he stopped, took a deep breath, and slowly peered around into a dead-end: a room filled by a somewhat larger version of the interior door they had used to enter this wing. There was a man seated near it, apparently asleep with his eyes open for he did not move except to jerk periodically erect, then slump forward again. Kai studied the door, trying to imagine how it was hinged, but he could not be sure, so he retraced his steps at a soft lope, slowing to walk past the door into his sisters' room, and dropped back into a run toward the inner door to the security zone beyond.

Six windows.

❧

As he approached the door to the interior cavern, his resolve wavered and the slightest of doubts crept in upon him. There were still too many things he did not know about this place, too many unexplored and unrevealing doors behind which lurked he knew not what. Guards could be waiting anywhere. The door may not open. He did not know. Once this began, there was no turning back. His steps slowed slightly, but he did not hesitate, reaching immediately for the raised square. He would rely once again on his instincts, his ability to improvise. The door opened. The hallway beyond was deserted, except for the expected crossings and re-crossings of figures a long way down the hall.

He did not run again, but walked briskly and deliberately to the door with the lightening bolt, which also opened to his touch. Relieved, yet somewhat puzzled and apprehensive that all doors should open so easily to him, he stepped inside and slid to his left, his back against the wall.

His eyes grew quickly accustomed to the dim lighting and he could vaguely discern the shapes of the whining things, here and there, and the alcove where a man sat absorbed in something on the table in front of him. Getting this far had been simple, too simple, but now his ignorance was apparent. There was only one way to make certain, and there was no time to lose since Ursla would expect his immediate return. He moved toward the alcove.

The same man was there, stooped over the table, his back to the door. Kai stepped up behind him and locked the man's windpipe in the crook of his arm, simultaneously turning to his left. They hit the floor hard, Kai on top, but the man's wind was gone. Through shocked, fearful gasps, he was able to hear Kai, who tantalized him with short bursts of air by relaxing his grip periodically. He had no time for guile, no time for indirectness, and certainly no time to let the older, heavier man have a reprieve. "Tell me how to turn off the lights, or I'll kill you!" The man's eyes went even wilder.

"Lights?" He was buying time to think.

"All the lights. Where?" He tightened his grip; the man stiffened. "Tell where, or I will destroy all the things in this room." The man's panic went beyond his means to control it.

"No. No. It will kill everyone. They need air. Please. Please. O.K. O.K. Let me up."

This would be difficult. Kai's control over him was tenuous, and standing would put him at a momentary disadvantage, off balance. The man would have time to recover from his shock and lack of air. The man was slow, heavy and soft, but he could be dangerous in his fright. Kai moved to his left, keeping the pressure on with only one arm. He reached for the man's wrist, bent the arm at the elbow until the wrist came up between them, against the man's back where he could wrench it if necessary. At least he could throw him off balance if he tried to break free. Kneeling, he slowly rose with the man leaning into him. The hard part was over.

"First, the doors. Fix the doors." The man squirmed and tried to utter a "but." Kai could not waste more time with him. "The doors. Take their power away, now." He flexed harder with his arm, wrenched up with the other, and the man crumbled back against him, pointing toward the darkness outside the alcove. In the farthest corner where Kai had placed his hand on the cool surface of the machine, the man led him to a wall of dim lights. Here, he moved about, touching and pushing with his free hand.

"O.K." Kai pulled him back to the far wall, then the door, and told him to touch the raised square. Nothing happened. Satisfied, Kai dragged him back. "Now the lights." The man hesitated; Kai squeezed. A raised finger pointed the way. Again before a wall of things Kai could not comprehend, the man's free hand darted here and there until the only light left in the room came from small, weak beams along the floor.

Kai dragged the man back to the door, feeling his way from memory and with tentative feet. He let go the wrist and felt the smooth surface and seam of the door itself. He pushed the man back into the center of the room until he could spot what he needed, a flat piece of metal on a workbench near the door. He put the cold metal in his teeth, and slowly sank to his knees. The man's agitation grew, and Kai attempted only a brief glimpse under the door to insure there was no light coming under it from the hall.

He tightened his grip, and braced for the contest as the man fought for air, only to slip slowly, quietly into unconsciousness. When his body relaxed, Kai loosened his grip until he could catch the first faint rattles of breath return. He quickly stripped the material he used for a belt and tied the man's hands behind him.

Using the soles of his shoes and the right angles of the

door, he turned one end of the metal upward into a right angle, a hook. His fingertips hastily explored the lower edges of the door where he worked the angled edge of the metal underneath and then up, catching the far side with its hook. He heaved, and the door slowly came away from the jamb just enough for him to catch an edge and, using both hands, pry it open.

It was completely dark in the passageway, but he kept to the right wall using one hand on its surface to guide his way. He broke into a trot, his left hand extended in front of him and all his senses acutely focused on the obscurity all around him. The lights had been out only a brief time, but long enough certainly to alarm everyone and, he hoped, for the guard to have moved. In the distance he could hear screams and people yelling to one another in the dark.

His outstretched hand struck the hall's end where he searched for the door. He pushed; it gave way before him, grudgingly. In the shorter hallway, there was a dim light from the windows, beyond which the night lights outside provided their weak, minimal illumination. He could not see or hear anyone around him, so using his left hand to judge he counted the number of window lengths to the door. Pressing his ear to it, he could hear voices within, so he pushed gently. This door resisted more than the others, but it, too, finally gave way to his urgent strength. He kept it open only a short distance and, bracing to keep it in position, reached inside along the wall. His hand found a form, another's arm, then hand, and he pulled. She slid out through the crack in the doorway and put her mouth next to his ear immediately.

"Nata is not here. She is not coming."

There was no time to question, no way to go inside and change her mind, so he gave the door a push to free himself, then turned and trotted down the corridor, his sister's hand in his. At the corner he stopped and dropped into a crouch. Just in case, he peered around the edge into the darkness where he could hear the guard's breathing. He was pacing back and forth, nervous and alone. Kai hesitated just long enough to fix the door in his mind and to let go Lori's hand and to put his on her shoulder, squeezing the brief message for her to stay put. Then, he moved off into the oblivion.

He moved quickly and quietly along the right wall until he could feel the slight breeze from the guard's movements. He did not breathe, he did not stand, but simply reached out until he felt the first shin bump into his arm, then darted out with all his strength and both arms, tripping the guard facedown with a crash before he could gasp his surprise.

He swung one leg over and straddled his back. One hand searched for the hair, entwined it in his fingers, and wrenched the startled face upward, then forward, driving it into the floor. He prepared to do it again, but there was no need. All resistance was gone, so he called to Lori and scrambled to the door.

This one proved more difficult. Although similar to the others, it evidently had greater bulk. By himself, he could barely budge it, and after Lori found her way to him, the two could only gain a little more advantage. Slowly, agonizingly, they pushed forward, it hissing its disapproval. Kai, working near its edge, used the piece of metal to wedge into the gap to keep them from losing the little ground gained with each heave, each followed by a brief gasp for air, and then another, more desperate push until he thought his muscles would explode.

It seemed impossible, until the image of his family came to him as if carried on the light night breeze so softly blown through the thin crack of the door. He and his sisters had been gone for days, and now a sharp image of his mother and brother found this moment. And the thought of her grief, then her glee at the return of her children gave him a surge of strength from deep within. The voice in him screamed that no obstacle could stop him.

He heaved and held, then rolled to his back to wedge his arm and leg through for a brace against the outside wall. Putting his back and shoulder through, he found the leverage he needed and the door opened slowly until there was enough for a passage. He felt her body slip by him and in the dim light from above he could see the shape of Lori outside, so he, too, sprang free of the door which stalled, then hissed shut behind him just as he was struck from behind by the rush and dive of someone against him.

He was wrestling with a demon clutching at his throat from behind with deep and metallic claws and he reacted instinctively, bring his clinched fist upward over his shoulder at the outstretched head with its whirl of hair, rolling as he did. His knuckles connected with the point of the jaw, driving the head upward and sharply back against the tension of the arms encompassing Kai's neck. The force behind the rush against him was immediately transformed into a limp falling away toward the ground as the form dropped heavily from him like a discarded robe, but not before Kai caught a glimpse of the face within the flurry of hair tossed back by the blow.

Breathing heavily, he rolled Ursla over carefully. Her breath was irregular and labored as her body twitched. "How did she get out?" He looked to his sister.

"I'm not sure. She must have figured out your plan." He hoped that was how it happened. If not, he may have missed something like another door, or another possibility for getting out of the mountain, and this could ruin their hopes of an escape.

"Come on. We have to get going, now. Can you remember the trail down?" She nodded and started toward the lip of the incline before them, but as they moved away, Kai stopped cold. Yes, it said to him. Yes.

It somehow made perfect sense, so he returned to Ursla and hoisted her limp figure over his shoulder. Her head came to rest against his lower back, bobbing occasionally into it as they worked their way down the steep and uneven slope in the dark. Kai labored under his load, and under the fears that the raiders could see even in the dark, that they had repaired the lights too soon and now knew of their escape and that they even now followed their progress down the mountain.

Chapter Nine

# Turning Tails

And they were. By the time the three had covered only a short distance the first alarms in the mountain had turned into action as ancient procedures and contingency plans were resurrected haphazardly from dim recollection. Some of the people were prepared, so doors gave way. Hands grasped weapons in the darkness, groping for the outside.

Lights came on, but on the bare slopes of the mountains, there was no indication. Windows emitted no light, walls deadened all sound, but Kai knew. He assumed they were angry, and he felt the flurry of action as if vibrations from the ground itself. His advantage would be only momentary and pursuit was certain. They had no weapons. They were vulnerable and weak. He had only partially planned the rest, so now his blood pumped harder, a drumbeat driving him to exceptional efforts of mind and body in unison. Dawn was a ways away, and although he required light, he would have to do without for now.

Within the mountain, a momentary establishment of order soon fell apart. Serious decisions needed to be made, but there was no Director. Chaos reigned as the search for her lengthened with no results, and then above the din in the security zone, the voice of Lorn was heard, and obeyed.

As they neared the tree line Kai slowed and looked first for the intersecting trail and then the patch of saplings. Their lighter color stood out from the darkened background. Lowering Ursla to the ground, he told Lori to watch her closely and then moved cautiously off the trail, keeping low to the ground. How many days? How long since the day the glider died, there, above that ridge? So much had changed that it seemed long ago that he had first stood on this spot.

He found a stick, and this helped. He prodded the ground ahead of him with it, and when its dried wood produced a metallic ring, he stooped to work the ground loose from around the base of the booby trap, prying it from the dirt like a ripe vegetable. In a short time, working briskly but cautiously, he had harvested six of the sharp-spiked, fake flowers and had an open path back to the trail. Carrying three by their shafts in each hand, he wound his way back to Lori. Two he planted by the trail, close to its lip and leaning inward, one on each side. He then showed Lori how to carry them, and why she had to be careful. He grunted as he lifted Ursla to his shoulder. His sister hesitated.

"But, are these necessary? These people are not so bad."

"We need to slow them, and I assume that, for them, these are not deadly. Besides, who planted them here, and for what purpose?" He moved down the trail, Lori immediately behind him but silent in thought.

On the infrared sensors above—slowly being re-calibrated after their loss of power—their pause was assumed to be a rest. However, their motions were still vague and distorted, and the actual number of escapees, uncertain.

As Kai set the next two—staggering them and leaning them out from behind the trunks of the first stunted trees—Ursla revived. At first, she sat groggily shaking her head from side to side in the middle of the trail, and then blinked unwittingly around her at a loss to explain who or where she was. Lori spoke to her first, quietly and gently, but she did not comprehend until Kai returned and stepped into her field of vision. He eased her gently to her feet and she moved off with them, complacently at first, when he said they must move quickly. He had seen the first lights of a search party appear on the peak above.

They had covered half the distance from the rockslide to the base camp below when Ursla made her first attempt. She slowed, letting Kai get several steps ahead before she swung around on Lori. But the young woman had seen her slow and had anticipated what was to come. She was ready. The blow glanced from her shoulder as she twisted and ducked, then dove forward, driving the same shoulder into Ursla's unprotected stomach. They went over, Lori on top groping for the wrists she intended to pin to the ground.

As Kai worked to untangle them Ursla became more frantic in her efforts. For a moment, he considered striking her again, but now, with time to think rather than simply react, he decided against it. She was doing exactly what he would be doing in her position: striving for freedom. Courage should not be answered with blows, but she was strong and it took both of them to subdue her. Finally, all three panting in the center of the trail, the silence dropped once more about them, and they heard the scream.

It was high-pitched and awful and clear in the quiet of the night. It was fear, anger and pain, at once, and it was bitten off. The sudden quiet, the peaceful gurgling of the stream below in the bottom of the canyon seemed oddly out of place and hollow for that one instant, or perhaps it was the drama transpiring on the mountainside above them that was hollow, he thought. Kai felt a shudder creep over him, and he wished deeply and passionately that he had not needed to use the traps. But he also knew that they would move very cautiously now, and this would slow them and give his small party an advantage. Things had been reversed.

"She's going to slow us down."

Kai nodded. Even in the darkness he could sense her. She was turned back up the trail, reading the significance of that scream, and he could almost see the hatred that was beginning to edge and harden her beautiful eyes. She would indeed be difficult, but now he saw clearly the edge he had from her capture and abduction. "We need her. They won't attack us while we have her. Besides, I think Luther would like to talk with her, the leader of the raiders, face to face." He felt Lori's interest shift back to their prisoner, and Ursla stiffen under his grip.

"You'll never make it back. They'll catch up with us, you know. It would be best if you turned back. You won't be harmed, either of you. I promise."

"We need something to tie her arms with. I used my belt already. Give me yours."

"I have something even better." Lori produced a fist-sized roll from within the folds of her short robe. Grasping one end, she let the roll fall loose to the ground, and then began tying Ursla's arms behind her with the strap. When she finished, she held the tether as a leash. Kai tested the thong, and then looked to Lori.

"It's the same one they used on us. I hid it away when they took it off and made us bathe and change clothes. Someone left it on a table and I thought I might use it. You know, just in case."

Kai smiled. She was strong and smart and resourceful, like their mother. The tether was pliable yet very strong. "It is like the metal. No wonder I couldn't cut it. We have to go." He motioned them on, picking up the last two booby traps after the two passed by him. He looked back up the trail, and then dropped one where it could be easily seen. He did the same with the last one, farther along. They had been slowed and warned. Perhaps all they needed was a reminder.

They made good time now that Ursla was confined. However, despite the bonds, she made one last dash when they arrived at the base camp, kicking Lori off balance and ripping the tether from her grip with a sudden, violent spurt away from the trail. She almost made it to the rocks before Kai caught up, grabbed the loose thong, and jerked her roughly to the ground.

She could have cried in her frustration and anger, but she did not. "I know you have to try. But, please, make it easier on yourself. You won't get away, and remember that there are traps out there, and, down there, where the traps end, there are dangers just as deadly." He did not specify. He implied, hoping her lack of knowledge of his world would kill her enthusiasm and help control her, just as his had controlled him in hers. They returned to the trail and continued, picking up their pace.

Dawn found them far beyond the raiders' territory, far past their last surveillance point. Although more comfortable, Kai was too smart to feel relieved. They had made it farther than he had actually hoped when he hastily made his escape plan, and this early success allowed him time to develop the next stage of their flight. They were tired, and Lori's fatigue wore heavily upon her. He knew she would go until she dropped, without protest or whimper, so he decided to make the change here. The raiders would make better time during the day. It was impractical to believe they could not catch up, so he hoped their confidence in their power would work for him, that they would be too intent on the chase, and that they would not have good trackers.

He stopped them near a curve in the trail. "Sit. Rest. I'll be right back." On the inside of the curve there were rocks, so he stepped on these and moved off into the brush to the west. That was the direction of the other trail, the one the raiders had used on their return to the mountains after the raid. He had purposely used the old, direct trail to the villages they had used, themselves, hoping they would consider his destination obvious and not pay too close attention to the trail itself.

He found a tight grove of short tree seedlings where they could rest but remain unseen from the trail. He returned and led the others to it, making sure there remained behind no trace in the dirt of their leaving the trail. If they were lucky, very lucky, no one would notice that their prints suddenly disappear. Only an experienced tracker could single out their tracks from all the others from the raiding party; the sandals all three of them wore might work in their favor. To an untrained eye, they would be indistinguishable from the previous party's. As a precaution, Kai made sure there was an easy escape route out of the grove and into the forest.

He awoke at mid-morning suddenly tense and alert. His fatigue dropped from him as he scanned back up the trail. They were coming; he could feel it and the inside voice was confirming it. He could not hear them yet, but sensed their presence from the silence that traveled with them as the forest listened, then broke into its noisy exchange after they had passed. He looked to Lori. She was awake, too, and looking in the same direction. He put his hand gently over Ursla's mouth. She awoke slowly and when her eyes finally opened, he applied more pressure to make his point clear.

There were five of them, three dressed as the earlier party and equally armed. There had been more the night before as they left the city. Although he could not count the lights accurately, there had been more than five. One had been wounded. Perhaps one or two had returned with her, but even with these losses, there should have been more. Were they so confident in their superiority? Or, and this thought chilled him to the core, had they divided their forces to cover both trails? He had been very careful to leave plenty of indication to the trail he had taken, but had they planned ahead? Had they considered the not-so-obvious possibility he was smart enough to use their own logic? If so, they had already adapted to his influence, and he and his sister were probably doomed.

The group did not slow at the curve, but forged on steadily. No one looked to the ground, or to the brush for that matter, so intent were they upon their goal. When he was sure they had moved on, he relaxed his grip on Ursla's mouth, but kept his hand in its place. A shout would carry a long distance, and she had squirmed enough as they passed that he had unconsciously slid on top of her to suppress her movements. Now, he looked down into her face and saw, even in her hatred, a softening. "I'm sorry Ursla. I hope all this comes out well, for both our people. Believe me." He rolled off her. "Now we have to move. I'm not sure which trail is shorter, but we have to beat them to the village. The people must be warned."

He led the way this time through the forest, quietly, choosing their way carefully with one eye on the sun and the other on the trees' shadows. The west trail was closer than he had expected. It caught him by surprise when he stepped into it where it curved toward them.

He motioned Lori and Ursla into a crouch and moved back along the curve to look up the trail, and when satisfied it was deserted in that direction, he moved back to the other end of the curve and looked for tracks. His own from days before were still clearly visible, superimposed upon the older ones of the raiders. He knew where he was. They had a long way to go and they would have to hurry.

So intent was Kai upon the trail behind that he almost ran into Ursla's back when, later that afternoon, Lori halted abruptly in her tracks. She was in the lead because Kai took the rear, fearing surprise from that quarter from the other half of a split party pursuing. He was shocked by their stop and moved up close to Lori.

"There is someone coming up ahead."

He nodded toward the brush on their left. As a precaution, he placed his hand over Ursla's mouth again. "Don't make a sound!" He then heard the movement ahead, and led them behind a large tree with a tight undergrowth of short bushes.

He was beginning to gain a bit more respect for these foes, who could anticipate and react. Obviously, the five had finally seen there were no fresh tracks on the trail and realized where they had gone, and now had them cut off and trapped between their two forces. His mind raced, but it could find no resting point that would provide another plan for escape, other than luck.

If they passed, there was still a chance. If they saw the tracks, they would know where to look. There had been no time to cover them, to obscure where they had left the path. And he was so intent upon his search for alternatives and routes of escape that he relaxed his grip upon Ursla's mouth, and that was all she needed.

In one swift motion, she shook her mouth free enough to clamp her shiny white teeth onto the heel of his hand, and then quickly released it as his reflexes jerked it away. Her scream was not as loud as she had hoped, but it carried far enough. By the time he wrestled her still again and had regained his grip over her mouth, there was an ominous silence on the trail.

Frantic to escape, he looked around him, and then behind, directly into Shawn's drawn, taut bow and a sharp arrowhead.

Chapter Ten

# A Leader Is Born

His uncle could not, or would not, hide his joy over Kai and Lori's return. He wept, openly. He sprang from one to the other and back again to hug them, and to laugh through his tears at his own lack of control. At first uncomfortable from such an emotional welcome, Kai warmed with each touching and, briefly, he felt his worries and fears slip away. His uncle was a powerful man and this moment was so very necessary, so historic. Although far from his village, they were home.

And Ursla felt it too. Initially crestfallen that her scream should have the opposite effect of what she had hoped, she stood straight and met her captors eye to eye. She did not flinch as she was led into the mass of half-naked men, or when the crowd closed tightly around them. Her arms ached from the strap, she was tired and sore, but she held her shoulders back and did not turn from their curious stares.

His uncle was a powerful man, but one burdened by age and the things it brings. Power is a demanding force, and his greeting completed with Kai and Lori, Luther turned his full attention upon Ursla. He returned her defiant sneer with a smile, a slight nod of his gray head and, turning to

159

Kai, a look of pure inquisition.

"When we return to the village, you must tell me of all that has happened, all that you have learned, but for now, I assume that you fear being chased. Come, we will talk about it and about your missing sister." Before he left Ursla, however, he put his hands on her shoulders and, pulling his strength together, he tried to dull her pain. "Rest now. You are safe with us. We mean you no harm. Eat. Rest." He nodded to two men standing behind her. In response, they untied the strap, marveled at its material, and reached into their bags for dried meat as they guided her a short distance off.

Kai put his dilemma before the men and Luther as quickly as possible, telling them only those details immediately necessary for their escape. When he told of the possibility of two groups, one on each trail, Luther interrupted to send men to watch the trail above, and others to guard the trail below. Before they could leave, Kai told them of the weapons and their terrible force. The situation was dangerous, and clear, and they needed a plan, but one had slowly taken shape in Kai's imagination as things unfolded and now, as they talked, it took a heavier, a more probable form. However, he needed to tell them more, if it was to work.

"There is something else. I know why our people have failed before when they have gone into the mountains." He told them of the traps, of the raiders' ability to see the whole mountainside from the safety of their home. He did not tell of the city inside. Not yet. Not here.

"And the clothes they wear, they are very, very strong. They can stop an arrow shot at close range. But, they can be killed." He told a brief version of his first encounter, and with it came the same revulsion, the same despair and terrible longing, as if he were living it again, only more clearly and slowly, or as if the telling helped him understand his own life and actions, for once.

His uncle did not miss an inflection or hastily chopped image or nervous lilt in Kai's voice. This, too, must be dealt with soon, he thought.

"As I told the others, their weapons are powerful. If they see us, they can kill us, and they are on the way to the village. They get closer as we talk." He fell silent, suddenly drained, exhausted after dropping his lonely burden on the communal shoulders. Around him, the men's eyes were wide with wonder and amazement, but also gleaming with hope as never before. Now they knew more of their enemy, that he was like them, mortal and no more.

"What do you propose to do?" His uncle's simple appeal told the whole story. Kai had been elevated to an advisory role, perhaps even to leadership, despite the fact that he was still a child, an uninitiated thing. In this brief flash of recognition, he understood more deeply the ways of his people. Initiations were complex and difficult, awesome things because they needed to be in times of peace and comfort. In extraordinary times, extraordinary actions took their place, and from them came new types of initiations. And there were the new stories that came from these times of trauma and joy. It all made sense.

"I see men from several villages here. How many are we?" Luther told him. "Good. First, we need to protect the village, and I am not sure we can get there in time to do much to prepare. Even if we ran, they still have a good lead. So, I propose that we split our forces and slow them. One group could run this trail until they are ahead of the raiders I saw, cut them off; another could go back up toward the mountains to meet the others that must be coming. We need to prepare ambushes. They walk very blindly in their arrogance. If we surprise them, we can use our weapons, rocks and clubs to knock them off balance. Perhaps, we can get more hostages, some of their weapons." There was a murmur of approval among the men, but Luther frowned.

"And your captive?" He would see how fully Kai had thought through this bold plan.

"She is strong, and determined. She would reveal an ambush." His cheeks flushed at his own shame. She had certainly revealed his own hiding place, in front of these very men. "A few men could take her down this trail, slowly. She would be safe, and her guards could act as a backup to those on the other ambushes. Afterward, we can all meet on the east trail before the village . . ." He did not finish the other possibility, that only a few men were actually committed to fights and if things went badly the rest might have time to escape with loved ones from the village, if they could, before the raiders destroyed it.

"And you?"

"I would like to go with the group ahead to stop the five closest to the village. My experience may be useful."

"Good. You lead that group. You have dealt with these raiders. You know." But Luther did not need to justify his call. The men saw clearly the logic of Kai directing the ambush. "And I will stay with this group. I am old and need to rest. I could not run ahead. I slow us down as it is. Ask these men how I drag." But there were hidden smiles all around. He had moved beyond fatigue, and age and pain as he drove them all relentlessly after Kai's disappearance from the village had been discovered. Kai knew that the old man took what he thought to be the most difficult stand, if there was indeed a large force coming down from the mountain.

The decision made, the preparations were brief, as it must be when everyone knew the dangers and the necessity to hurry. Kai took leave of Lori, holding her close a long while. He respected his sister, and, now, she had survived a terrible ordeal, and prevailed, and he loved her for that, too. She had done well on their escape. And he thought sadly of Nata, left alone above in the mountain. "Good luck, sister. Our mother waits." She nodded, and then looked away.

He went to Ursla, but there were no words. Instead of stammering through stupid sounds, he simply touched her shoulder and looked her directly into the eye, then quickly turned and set off at a trot down the trail toward the village. Without a word, almost without a sound, the men fell in behind him.

They set their ambush the next morning. They had kept their pace well into the night, slowing to a walk only to rest, and to eat. When they did stop, it was to drink only, and then only briefly. They cut back through the forest, two scouts well in advance, and cut the other trail far away from the village and well ahead of the raiders. The only tracks were old and mostly obscured.

Kai had a place in mind. He and Shawn and their childhood warriors had once used it in a mock war, a war that was now very real. It was nicely suited. There were many places to hide as the trail skirted a hill. Half his men could be there, with the up-hill advantage and abundant rocks for cover. Others would crouch close to the trail, but below. There were boulders and trees enough for a few who could be positioned to jump the raiders from behind. With a bit of inexperience working against the raiders, and with luck, perhaps they would be unprepared, and easily overwhelmed.

Not always a firm believer in luck, Kai sent two men to the village to warn the people, and then to watch the trail. Should the raiders not be surprised, these men would clear the village. He sent two more back up the trail to watch for their coming. One would return with the news, and one would follow the party, in case. Then Kai positioned five more, high above the trail in each direction. If anyone slipped by the ambush, they would cut them off and act as reserves.

Finally, he set the ambush itself: four below, himself included, and the rest above the trail. These were staggered to avoid arrows or rocks hitting their own men. Although those above would draw the first fire, the rocks there were big and offered safe cover. One could avoid a blast. But below, this he saw as the greatest danger. To jump a raider, one had to step into the open, become exposed to their weapons. If the weapons did not get you, one of your own men might hit you by mistake. But it was necessary to be close: a dropped weapon must be grabbed immediately, a fallen raider disabled. They must create confusion and panic if they were to live.

The scout returned too soon, long before Kai had expected him.

"They were only a short distance away—near the pond with the stinking water. They must have walked all night, too. They look very tired."

The unexpected need for haste bothered Kai, but there was nothing to do for it. There was no time to reconsider, or to worry over every little detail. If there had been, he might have better understood the raider's reasoning, their all-night drive for the village. As it was, he rushed his men into place with only half-spoken orders, walked up the trail to be sure no one could be seen where they hid, and brushed the trail clean of tracks with a cut branch. Then, he took his own place, near the first rocks. If the ambush were discovered, he would draw the first fire and give the others time to adjust—to attack, or retreat.

The lead raider was nearly through the curve and free of the trap when Shawn rose and hurled a huge stone directly at her. Never an accurate thrower, but a powerful one, Shawn missed, but the shock value of his appearance worked, and the rock, on the bounce, took the raider's left leg, striking just below the knee. And then there was a flurry of rocks and shouting and wild, short-lived chaos accentuated only by three blasts from the weapons, followed by the acrid stench of smoke and burnt wood and stone.

Kai crouched lower on the downhill side of the trail as the rocks rolled off, driving one raider to cover directly into Kai's clinched fist. Plunging around the boulder Kai was using for cover himself, the raider's attention had been drawn by an accurately thrown rock in the middle of the back. Kai simply sprang from his crouch using the force of his legs to propel his fist. It took the raider on the chin, crumpling and falling to the right, releasing the weapon from senseless fingers. It was that simple. Kai scooped up the weapon and stepped into the trail just as the hail of rocks ceased. Two raiders lay in the open; another was on the ground below the trail with two of Kai's men on top. Beyond, a small fire burned near Shawn's hiding place.

"Shawn!" The man's head peeked above the charred boulder, wild-eyed.

"I'm OK."

"Where is she?" Shawn pointed a tentative finger in the direction of the forest on the downhill side of the path. Kai looked at his weapon. How did it work? He could tell which end fired its deadly blast, but how to make it work? There was risk in using it too soon, if he went into the tangle of brush after Shawn's wounded raider. He signaled the men to take cover and, keeping low, he weaved his way to Shawn.

"She?"

"Get to the men down trail and cut off the way to the village, just in case. Which way should we look?"

Shawn waved toward the canyon. "There, below the biggest tree, that is where the blast came from. The raider slid down that dirt slide and, there, shot the last time. The leg I hit might be broken."

"Good. The trail is safe then. Get the men, and work your way back in the direction of the village, but be careful. You see what they can do." He needn't have warned his friend. The impression had been made, and Shawn's affected valor had been tempered under fire.

Kai stepped below and had the men gather the weapons

and prisoners. All were alive, but one had a serious head wound, which was bleeding badly, and one had a broken leg just above the ankle. As he walked among them, he stopped suddenly cold, for the first time aware of the obvious. They were all men, all the raiders, yet Ursla had told him the raiding parties were always made up of women. The unexpected once more, Kai thought, and he felt his uneasiness dull his initial sense of victory. Something was happening. Something was going to come of this change, and it worried him.

Anxious to return to the larger party and report, but also to talk of this with Ursla, he busied himself seeing to the litter building for the wounded raider. Before he could leave, however, there was a blast from below the trail. Several tense moments later, two of his men emerged from the brush.

"Shawn says no one is hurt badly, so you must not worry. Tamar got a small wound in the thigh, but he will be fine. We got a little too close. The raider is hurt, but he seems to be heading back toward the mountains. We have him blocked from the village, so Shawn wants to know what we should do. Go after him?"

Kai gave it a moment's careful consideration. One person alone and hurt could be dangerous if pressed, as well he knew. Like any wounded animal, they can be deadly if cornered. He could be mild, however, if his escape route is left open and time wears upon his wound. "Let him go. Hold where you are until dark, then go to the village."

Feeling a bit more relaxed, Kai returned to preparations. "You will be safe on the trail. Finish building your litters there, but first, remove the clothing from the prisoners. Leave some of it, spaced, on the trail. If others come, this may give them something to think about, and maybe slow them down. We have hostages now, too."

As he and two others turned to the forest and toward the other trail, he took one last look over his shoulder. Men, all men the voice kept repeating. He was thankful that he had not told his men they would be fighting women. This might have subtly altered their reactions, and perhaps the outcome of the confrontation. Even the slightest hesitation might have cost them, and Kai knew all too well that these women were a match for them, if not superior. Now, they had tasted their first victory against these people. But would there be others? Would there be the need for other battles?

When they reached the west trail, they broke into an easy lope, trying to narrow quickly the distance between them and the other ambush. However, they had been too long on the march and there had been too much tension and too much thought with too little sleep. The lope slowly dissolved into a steady, determined plodding into evening.

By the time Kai had resolved to rest for the night and proceed again just before dawn, they came upon the guards, Lori and Ursla. They, too, had had a long march and were looking for a place of concealment for a camp. Together, the two groups moved off the trail into a small opened meadow, leaving two for guards, one below and one above, to watch the trail.

Kai noticed that Ursla's arms had been tied behind her again. Feeling it safe to let her free with so many eyes to watch her, he loosened the straps. Throughout the process, she did not look at him. She had not said a word since the two groups joined. As he rolled the strap once again into a fist-sized mass, Lori came up behind him.

"She tried it again, this morning early. She was gone only a little while, but if she had a few moments more, she could have gotten to the other trail."

He nodded, and then fell silent, gazing at Ursla's back. Lori drew off. She was hungry and tired and there were enough others to worry about the captive.

"So, you got away, but made for the obvious goal. To warn your party? Too late. But you are resourceful, and responsible. We're a lot alike."

She pivoted slowly on the large rock she had chosen for her seat. She studied him a minute. Like her, he was tired but there was also a glow, a radiation in him that had not been there in the mountain. Its presence was both perplexing, and threatening, but she had begun to understand it, and herself.

"I see you have new weapons. So, you murder us for better ways of killing. Did you sneak up upon them in their sleep?" Her voice had a sarcastic edge to it, and although he felt sympathy, perhaps even empathy, for her, it grated upon him. He rose to his feet, made sure there were men sitting in each direction, and then looked down upon her.

"We set an ambush, and they walked into it on their way to attack my village. We stopped them. We took them prisoner. The tactic should be familiar to you." He moved slowly off to the trail. He would check on the guards, but first . . . "And no one died." The emphasis had its effect. She fell silent and turned abruptly away.

In the morning they prepared to continue their separate

ways, until one guard brought a runner from Luthor's group.

"They didn't come. No one came down the trail from the mountain. We went back toward the mountain as far as we felt safe, and sent scouts ahead. They went all the way to the base where the trails separate. No one else had come down, except the five you saw." Like Kai, he was at a loss to explain it. Ursla's people had plenty of time to react, but with only five? Could they still be so arrogant in their superiority? But, like Luther, he was willing to accept the facts and plan accordingly. They would return to the village, content that the raiders had assumed they would catch up with Kai and Ursla before they got to the village, and that five well armed people would be sufficient for their task. But something nagged him about it, and he hoped to stifle the voice within him so that he could join in the joy of the others. A first victory? Or only an insignificant first skirmish?

After their jubilation died down, Kai concluded that there was no need to join with his uncle's group. That would require a long wait where they were, so instead he sent the runner back to Luther, telling him that they would wait for his arrival short of the village, near the river. They could all go in together. He also warned him of the wounded raider trying to make his way home.

Once the runner had departed, the rest turned toward the village. There was a lightness in their going, a lightness tempered by the fact that no one believed their ordeal was over, only postponed. Ursla walked without bonds near the middle of the group, Kai near the front, fingering the strange weapon and trying to decide how it worked.

Their walk did not take long, or perhaps it was simply that the homeward trek was lost in their thoughts of family and friends and therefore did not seem to take long. As they camped that evening near the stream, several people came from the village to meet them and to stare at the captive. The other prisoners had arrived much earlier and had been taken directly into the village so that their wounds could be better tended, but they were silent men, and this new one was an oddity—a young woman, and a leader. The curiosity was too great, and although all would enter the village together ceremoniously upon Luthor's return, some of the more brave defied custom for a brief glimpse of Ursla.

One of these was Sadi, Kai's mother. No amount of persuasion or reasoning would have kept her at home in the village when two of her lost children were within a quick, easy walk. She was one of the first to arrive, tentative initially but then she swept into the camp on a wave of emotion. Kai and Lori tried to hug her gently, gingerly, because of her wounds, but she wouldn't allow this. She was beyond the physical pain that was constant from her broken arm, bound carefully against her torso to diminish movement. Her joy and tears were equally balance with a questioning look.

"She's back there, in the mountains with the raiders, but she is fine. They are not mean, or beasts. She is well treated and well fed, and unharmed. She is safe." It sounded hollow to Kai, even as he said it, but Lori picked up the chorus, recognizing her brother's obvious reserve and its implications.

"It's true. They're kind. They'll leave her alone." The strength of both having said it seemed to put her at ease, but Sadi noted her young ones' odd speech and began to consider the subtle ways change comes.

So they sat and talked—the adventures of the two never quite believable, their words to describe what they had seen never quite sufficient. Then, they moved together toward Ursla who was surrounded by a group of villagers whose curiosity had been amplified by the discovery that she could talk, that she could speak their language.

They will be even more confused when all is revealed, Kai thought. For now, however, it was enough to rescue Ursla and protect her from questions and bother within their small family. But they shouldn't have worried because it was getting dark and there was work to be done. The people brought wood from the village; they started fires and cooked food as a light and festive mood grew among them.

In the twilight, Kai took two men and moved a short ways from the camp. There was a rock outcropping near the stream and he had chosen this place to experiment with the weapon. He could have waited, and no doubt Luther would insist that he should wait until he arrived, but Kai knew that it would certainly have to be done, sooner or later. They might be able to persuade one of the prisoners to show them how it worked, but that was dangerous in more ways than one. They could not be trusted. Besides, to wait would put someone else in jeopardy, someone else behind the weapon and at risk.

Kai had come to feel responsible for this whole ordeal, this whole dilemma, this new and renewed threat, so he also felt responsible for meeting it. He would test the weapon now, and it would be done, and perhaps the sooner the better. Another raiding party may be on its way. They would need to prepare to meet them.

He positioned the men in trees well behind him, one on each side to observe what he did. If he failed, they would be able to report what he had done to make him disappear in a blast of fire. He told them what he knew for fact about the weapon, and what he had surmised from studying it. He knew so little that this did not take long.

Then he stood, alone, looking to a large boulder low down on the outcropping. He looked behind him, back toward the camp, took a deep breath, and brought what appeared to be a brace on the rear end up to his shoulder. When he lightly pulled the lever on the lower side of the weapon, nothing happened. He pulled it harder. Still nothing. He let out his breath. There were two raised, round surfaces on the sides. One was red. He took another deep breath and, aiming at the rock again, pushed this. It did not fire, but it began to emit a low, barely audible hum.

He sat the weapon down carefully and walked quickly back to the others. From behind a tree they watched and waited as he explained what he had done. When the hum did not increase in pitch or intensity, as it did that night back there on the hill before it exploded, he returned cautiously to it.

Picking it up, he studied it once again. He took aim, and touched the lower lever again. The flash blinded him. There had been sounds, too, a sudden rending of the air and a rise in the pitch of the hum. He did not notice these. The brightness of the flash alone had his full attention. Still slightly blinded, he lowered the weapon. Its low hum diminished as the other two came slowly up behind him.

"This thing is evil." The man's whisper was as powerful as a shout in the returning darkness. Kai turned. They all looked hastily around them, as if guilty of some terrible crime and afraid that some avenging being might step from the night to strike them dead for having tampered with forces beyond their comprehension, and need.

The thing in Kai's hands hummed contentedly away. He pushed the red button again. It hummed on. He pushed the one next to it and it fell silent. He looked at his companions. He could see the same confusion in their eyes. *What have we done?* The voice murmured quietly in his head. They returned silently to camp. In the night, the three huddled a little closer to the fire than usual, which they built to abnormal proportions. The festive mood was oddly dampened.

Ursla spent the night sleeping between Lori and Sadi, one ankle securely tethered to Lori's. Luther and his group arrived at mid-morning looking tired but still jubilant. Everyone's spirits picked up a bit at the reunification and with the preparations to enter the village.

First, they moved toward the stream to bathe, but as Kai led Ursla to a pool upstream from the large pool near camp in which the men would bathe, he felt a sudden and odd sensation, followed by a prickling of his scalp. He motioned her to stop. He wanted to wait for Lori, who had returned to camp for a piece of soap. They had no sooner stopped and he had only begun to move back toward her, when he heard it, a low hum off to his left in the brush. He did not have time to warn her, nor to complete his plunge toward her.

The weapon's blast spun her completely around, and the momentum of her body trying instinctively to escape the pain carried her a few steps before she toppled, face first, into the exposed dirt of the well worn trail. Kai reached her only after she lay still. Without thinking of the danger lurking in the brush, he knelt to tend to her. There was a burnt hole in the back of her tunic above the left shoulder near the neck. There was little blood. He rolled her gently over. She was unconscious and her face, now relaxed, appeared strange, unfamiliar to him. Her beauty struck him like an ax, and he prayed deeply that she would not die. He started to raise her before the reality of their situation came back. He let her slip back to the ground, noticing as he did her clinched fist.

In a flash, he knew clearly what it contained.

A movement in the brush drew his mind from the memory, and he knew he must act fast. Withdrawing backwards into the brush along the trail, he looked for his opening. The villagers were coming from the camp and the raider's attention turned to them. Kai slipped toward the stream bank, where he turned toward the camp. There was a flash of light behind, and he could hear the shrieks of his people and visualize their fright.

He covered the distance to camp quickly and, scooping up the weapon, returned the quickest way along the trail, the thing humming in his hands. As he passed the prone people crawling into the shadows off the trail, his eyes began their search, but he did not slow.

The raider was leaning against a tree, looking down upon

Ursla's unconscious form. The weapon was in his hands. He raised it.

Kai emitted a high-pitched scream and fired simultaneously. The first shot went wide; the second came immediately behind it and caught the raider dead center, pinning him against the tree where he stood upright, then leaned, then fell face forward to the ground. The eyes that stared at Kai in that brief moment of recognition as they began to glaze over were familiar. They were Ursla's.

Kai moved cautiously in to remove the weapon from the open hand, noticing the blood and odd angle to the left leg as he did. The clothing was torn and stained, and as he removed the hood he found the verification of what he already suspected but could not understand.

It was Lorn, and he was dead. The bloody, crushed knee solved only one, simple mystery. There were others more perplexing.

There was confusion about what to do, but then Luther's voice rose above the din and argument and it was decided. While the men bathed, he and Sadi would tend to Ursla's wound, with Kai watching. They had little knowledge of such wounds, but their understanding of the human body, its needs and recuperative abilities, was great.

Once the burnt hole was exposed, it did not appear as life-threatening as they had feared at first. Lorn's aim had been faulty. It had hit her too high to cause extensive internal damage. And, then, the blast had simultaneously caused and cauterized the wound, so they busied themselves with cleaning and salving it, and preparing for the pain that would come when she awoke. In a brief moment of hope, Kai sent to the village, but the raiders' belongings did not contain any of the medicine they had used on his own wounds.

After all was done, Luther and Kai bathed too. Once cleansed, they meditated upon their recent past and in their silence contemplated courses of action. By then the large group was ready and they all entered the village as a unit, leaving the bulk of their bad thoughts and violent actions behind them, out there.

Once inside, there was great celebration and the dark mood lightened as children joined them, dancing, laughing, teasing. Kai's younger brother bounced at him from behind one house on the outskirts, almost knocking him down as the little arms entangled his thighs. Kai lifted him to his shoulders, and he rode their bouncing, Kai skipping his way into the heart of the village to the crumbled ruins of their holy place, across from the charred remains of the burnt home. There was, indeed, a lot left to do.

Chapter Eleven

# Wounds

In the days that followed, the village seemed to slip back into its simple, soothing routine, although twice the usual number of sentries was placed on hills and trails. The daily activities didn't cover the reality of a world changed and a sense of impending threat.

For Sadi, her home seemed once again full. She celebrated the return of her children, and privately mourned the loss of one to a fate she could not imagine. She also wished that Kai would spend more time with his family and less with the men and Luther. Although she knew his absence was necessary and that the elder men must hear all that he had seen and learned, she missed his presence at home where he had a calming effect on her guest and patient, Ursla.

Sadi moved around her small home in search of her awl, pushing her delicate hands into nooks and crannies to discover all the little possessions that made this her home. Kai. He had been gone such a short time to change so dramatically, and this worried her when she allowed herself time to think and worry. He had become so strong, yet compassionate, so aloof yet so full of his family and people. This kind of feeling had been missing in her home since the death of her husband, and this thought took her down paths she preferred not to travel. She gave up her search and set about making their breakfast.

So, while Kai spent his days telling every tiny detail of his story to the men, his family drew tightly about Ursla. She had come to the morning after she was wounded, dry mouthed and obviously in a great deal of discomfort. Kai was next to her in the gray before dawn, watching her. She shook off her immediate sense of disorientation and steeled herself against the pain. She gradually gained control of it, and Kai noticed this. He could empathize with her; he could still feel the searing pain of his own wounds so he respected her obvious strength.

She was new to all this—the world outside the mountain, the long and tiring marches, the pain that comes from an unprotected existence—but she adapted and endured and he found much to respect in that. Maybe even love. He also regretted that he did not have the medicine for her that had healed his own wounds quickly, so he offered his only near equivalent. He reached out and touched her right shoulder, the one nearest him, and as his fingers grazed, then settled upon her skin, there was a momentary flash, as of static electricity on a stormy day or joy at a stolen moment, and it spread into a glowing warmth that moved freely in both directions.

She bent her elbow and brought her hand up to cover his, and then with a great deal of effort, slid closer to the wall on her narrow bed. She took hold of his hand and drew him down beside her, cradling his head on her good, warm shoulder. His hair smelled of wood smoke, but also of the forest and the stream. She leaned her cheek against its soft cushion, and they slept.

It took three days before Kai found a way to tell her what had happened. At first, he did not want her to suffer any more pain, but the obvious need for the truth wore upon him. When he neared the end of his story when he had told it to the others, the men debated the significance of her wounding, so he waited for the correct time to reveal to her how she was wounded and, more importantly, who had done it.

The other captives had been questioned, but they remained silent, reticent. Obviously, the politics within the raiders' village were very complex, and since the people of Kai's village were already confused by current events, this attempted assassination merely blended in with the overall sense that great change was in the wind, and equally great revelations forthcoming. So, the village was content to wait for the moment to come, confident it its own abilities to survive, to make adjustments and take what measures were necessary at the time. And to enjoy each other and each moment until the time came to act, as it always does.

But in their governing body, in that tight and secretive group of select men where important matters were carefully and deliberately considered, chaos ruled. On his first appearance before them, Kai had revealed only the existence of the city within the mountain before he was cut short and dismissed when the men started to talk all at once. Luther had their attention, so he told Kai to return the next morning and in the mean time to retrace his tracks in his memory so that he could be very certain of every detail. Then Kai found himself standing alone outside Luther's house, where the group met now that the holy place was destroyed.

It was his turn to feel confused and lost. He had envisioned this moment and had imagined the shock and surprise on the faces of the men as he told them of the wonders he had seen in the city above. Now, he had been dismissed, sent home and rushed outside before he could even tell it all. Like never finishing his initiation, this was too much to bear from old men more used to sitting on their butts telling stories than traveling the real world. Why? Did they not believe him? Had he frightened them? And what would tomorrow bring, with his revelations about the sun inside a mountain? And the night lights. He looked up. They shone down into his awe and wonder here, too, but these were real. And he thought of the people inside the mountain. They, like their night lights, were fixed and unchanging. They never moved or altered. He walked toward home pondering the differences between people here, and there.

The next morning he woke late. Sleeping with Ursla had relaxed him, soothed him, and he enjoyed the luxury of the early morning. But the light touch of Luther pulled him from his pleasant dream of wide expanses, of complete solitude with Ursla beside him. He moved off the bed cautiously, leaving her to sleep through her pain. The two men moved toward Luther's, Kai chewing on a piece of fruit. They walked in silence and tense anticipation.

He talked for two days. First, he delivered a monologue, his story well considered and expressed. Then, he answered questions, the detailed nature of which grew increasingly puzzling for him. He grew tired. He became hungry. He was amazed that his words had so little effect on them. Finally, his head swam as, late on the second day, Luther called for a recess.

In all that time, they had only brief breaks to eat, relieve themselves, get a drink of water, or to stretch old bones and joints. Finally, Luther called for this halt, sending Kai from the house where he waited for only a moment before he was called back inside. The group was obviously greatly agitated, at last, and there was no attempt to conceal their excitement. However, Luther, as usual, was in complete control and, when he spoke, everyone else stopped and paid close attention. His brief speech was followed by another dismissal.

"You have done well, nephew. Very well. We are proud of you. Very proud. And we have decided what we must do, at least for now. First, tonight we will announce that your initiation is complete. Your ordeals outside have prepared you for responsibility, so they have in effect initiated you already. We need only make this fact public. So, welcome home, and welcome into adulthood." They each rose and hugged the astounded Kai.

"Since you know so much that we don't know, you must join this group. And at a very crucial time. Whether or not we reveal to our people our kinship with the raiders has yet to be decided. People have probably started to wonder about this. But, then again, our relationship with them seems about to change, too. This must be managed well. The people may need to know, but when? This may be the time we have waited so long to come. There seem to be signs, indications. We must see what happens, and be ready because things may happen quickly. However, we cannot tell for certain until we meet and speak with this girl you brought to us." There were nods of approval and murmuring throughout the room.

"This woman." Kai flushed at his interruption, but they had to know and they had to re-think their own ideas. His voice had been repeating this inside him without stop since they came back into the village, at once familiar but changed for Kai.

"This woman. But before we can talk with her, she needs to know more about us. We want you to teach her, you and your family, so go home and send Sadi here. In two days, you will bring Ursla here. Until then, give her freedom. Be kind and open. And listen to her carefully. In two days, once she knows us, we will talk with her, and the captured raiders, too. Perhaps, then, we will see why a father would want to kill his child. Go now. Until tonight."

On his walk home, Kai came to realize that he was not the same person, not the same boy of that other initiation night so long ago, but only a few days past. He was no longer a child, floundering in the darkness of his age and wrestling with his convictions while trying to figure out how to behave. He was not the same person. No longer the half-frightened boy, the faces of the elders did not make him uneasy. Instead, he began to see them, for the first time: their dedication and devotion and self-sacrifice. On that initiation night, he had been intimidated by the ways they had painted themselves and the ways they acted and talked. Now, he saw pattern and purpose, the blends of night and day, darkness and light, and here and there on cheeks or forehead, a sprinkling of night lights. They wore their world in personal ways that marked their responsibility to make it work, this world in paint, the dark and light perfectly balanced and given symmetry by the fact that humans saw the cosmos and took it into account.

No longer a boy, he saw, understood, and appreciated. His uncle could feel this, not in words, but below language on an empathic level bred through the long generations on this small sphere spinning through a dark universe, on a level that bonded one person to another, one generation to another, and led logically and rightfully to survival. They shared this inner voice, and they cared for one another: the one important thing out of which all others grew and which gave balance to their world and purpose to individual lives. He remembered his uncle's short speech after he had finished his story of the city in the mountain and now it had become tied to the ones Luther told the night of his initiation that, at the time, made little sense.

"It was long ago, in the beginning. Out of death came life. Out of the chaos walked our people. Out of the darkness we stood alone, and cared for the few others who stood with us. We were tempered with fire and destruction, and we survived." The old man's words were well used, Kai could tell, but they were more than a description, an incantation of sorts, spoken with conviction and deep resolve and emotion.

He now felt the confusion and dread of the times long ago, and they shaped his being, his idea of the universe and himself, what should and should not be allowed. Kai felt this all in one brief flash, and that conviction became his own. It was only right, and he saw the necessity of small groups like the elders, their words and concerns.

As he neared his home, he began to understand the odd questions after he had finished his story. "Now, tell us nephew, on that night of your initiation, you were left alone. Did you see anything, hear anything, before the attack?"

Kai had taken a deep breath and shifted his position a bit. Then, looking from face to face, he told them of the dream, being certain not to leave out details, a sense of emotion or shade of feeling he had on that vast, expansive plain. Then, he told of her approach, his hiding as she came, her death, the dirt in the clasped fist, the word: "Lights."

The men listened intensely; no one moved a muscle, so intent were they on what he said. There was a murmur as he finished the dream, and then a restless agitation. Luther shifted in his place, as if to speak, but Kai had not finished. "But uncle, there is more." The silence was abrupt, the men instantly more tense. He did not wait for effect, but hurried on to Lorn's attack, Ursla lying wounded on the trail, her hand clasping the dirt, Lorn's eyes glazing over in death. He told it all with equal thoroughness, and, this time, there was no murmuring, only dead silence as each man stared into himself.

"There is a crisis here. There is change coming. When we bring the girl, this woman, here and talk with her she may hold the key to what has happened, to what will happen." Kai was beginning to see how Ursla's original idea of contact between their worlds may play out after all.

In the morning, Kai awoke full of restless energy. As they

were eating breakfast, his mother looked up expectantly from her food as if she waited for him to say something. A smile spread across her face. She rose and hugged Kai to her. They stood that way for several moments before Lori and Lan clamored for their own chance to hug this new person in their home. They laughed and chattered as Ursla looked on, her curiosity mounting. Sadi noticed this as she sat back down at her place closest to the fire.

"Today, my son is a man." She spoke this with great pride—a verification that he had indeed survived childhood, and all her worries, to be accepted as an adult. Ursla's chuckle did not go unnoticed. Sadi looked at her first with a bit of anger, thinking she may be scoffing at their traditions, but then curiosity took over, followed by dawning comprehension. She looked at her son. She looked at Ursla again, and then to Lori. They had all found their plates and were intent upon their contents.

So much had changed, in so short a time. But that is how it happens, Sadi thought. That is how it is continued from one generation to the next. For the first time in a long while, she felt that her children would be OK after she was gone. Now, her son had a mate. "Come. Eat. There is a lot to do today." Her children were no longer who they once were. They no longer belonged solely to her.

"I'm sorry if I offended you, but I find your customs so . . . so strange here." Ursla was sitting on a low stool at the end of the table, eating slowly. Her wound ached and with the slightest movements it became a sharp and intense presence. "I'm sorry again, so unfamiliar would have been better. But look at what you must do to survive. You have to cook every meal, although you're hurt. You get water, care for the children, do practically everything while the men sing the night away only to sleep all day, or disappear into the forest. Does this seem right?"

Sadi looked at her curiously, and chose her words carefully. "Everyone needs to do something. What would we do without our work?"

"I see. There are a lot of things that can occupy our time. Why should work? Where I live, women are leaders, not slaves."

Sadi looked at Lori, then Kai. Their looks verified the truth of Ursla's words, but not their meaning.

"And we don't need to cook or wash or care for children. It's all done by machines, or by men." Sadi wondered at this. She did not know what "slave" meant. She had never heard the word before, but she began to guess.

"You let others care for your children? How do they know their parents? How do they learn? What do you do?"

"Of course, we lead. We make decisions."

"All of you?" Sadi shook her head slowly, and then took another bite. Luther had warned her about the raiders' strange ways, the things they worshipped and believed.

"Where do you lead? In which ways do you go, if you do not have your children and the others to guide you in your choices? We make decisions here, too."

"But who makes them, you or the men?"

"Some are made by the women, others by men. Man, woman, it makes little difference as long as they are made by those who care, and that they are well made. Here, we care for one another."

Ursla did not respond immediately, but instead thought back through the moments to the hugs and joy so apparent and sincere in Kai's changed status. The memory was a nice glow, but how deep was this caring? She wondered, then doubted. She knew people, and they were all alike, all moved by similar self-concerns. "But the men control everything. Who decides who gets what?"

Sadi sat befuddled. She looked to Lori again, and to Kai, but they simply shook their heads and kept their mouths shut. This was not their discussion, and their mother had lived much longer. They would not presume to interfere, even if they could think of something more to contribute. Sadi felt Ursla's need for an explanation, but she was so close, so much a part of these things, that she was at a loss to put them into words. "I guess we do. The women."

This stopped Ursla short. "The women?"

"I guess. We keep the food, the homes."

"O.K. I see. The homes. But where did you get this home?"

Sadi looked around again, as if suddenly aware of the walls and ceiling for the first time. "Why, from my mother. When I took a husband, the children's father, we lived here. When my parents died, it became ours, and one day it will be Lori's or Nata's . . ." And this name dropped a heavy silence upon the discussion. She sat chattering with the leader of the people who had beaten her, broken her arm and home, who now kept her daughter captive. She turned hard, and cold, and Ursla felt it and ate the remainder of her meal in silence, trying to wrestle her way through the paradox of ownerships.

For two days, Ursla watched their routines. Still too weak

to travel, she let Kai move her out into the light where she sat on the bench near the door as curious people filed by trying to look as if they were on their way to an important and urgent meeting, but catching every nuance of Ursla's appearance. In this way, the village came to know her and grow comfortable with her addition to their things to talk about as they ate their evening meals.

And for two days, she formed her impressions of the primitive society she had learned to dismiss as a child. The ways these people operated were more complex than she had been taught and as she talked with Sadi and Lori she started to form another sense of history. They were certainly related, her people and theirs, and the fact that they had evolved, or not evolved, as separate societies began to capture her full attention. There was something lurking just beyond her ability to identify it.

There were similar core ideals in each. There were similar fundamental concepts and emotions that made people do what they do, but there were also these sharp differences in life ways. This sparked her curiosity and that spark grew into a flame as she became more agitated about her inability to just get up and go home where, she hoped, she might be able to unravel her thoughts and resolve what for both societies remained the real and most pressing question: how do we fight the disease that may ultimately kill both communities?

On the second day while she and Kai sat outside together watching the procession of village people, she finally brought it up. "I need to go home. When the rescue party . . ."

"Raiding party."

"When the rescue party doesn't return, they will come."

"I don't think so."

"They will. What's more important is that I follow through on the plan to get our two people together to fight the disease."

Kai put his hand on her arm and squeezed it. "We are together."

"You know what I mean."

"I do. But it will happen. Just wait."

She steamed. There were several responses she considered, but then thought better of it. "We can't just sit here doing nothing."

"You sound like me."

"I don't understand."

"That's how I felt after you people took my sisters."

"You people? You people?"

"I'm sorry, your people."

"My people were only doing . . . "

"Let's drop it, OK?"

"Not OK. If I'm going to be held a prisoner . . ."

"You can leave any time."

"Can any of your slaves leave any time? You wanted to know why none of the women we rescue ever come back." She swept her one good arm around as if taking in the whole village. "Any questions now?" As she started to stand in her growing anger, her vision began to tremble and the daylight to intensify, and then everything went black.

That evening, they were called to Luther's house. Ursla was still weak, so a litter was sent and Kai walked beside it. However, when the men who carried it slowed outside the doorway, Ursla asked them to stop and then stepped from it to walk the last few steps on her own, without assistance.

She stood before the fire and the men, erect and undefeated. She did not wait for the formalities; hers was not a social visit.

"I assume you are in charge of this gathering." She looked directly at Luther. "I hope you'll finally answer some questions, honestly." His eyebrow fluttered upward. "No one here seems to want to tell me anything." She did not use Kai's name, and the exclusion was noticed.

"Please. Sit down. Make yourself comfortable. How is your wound? Is it painful?"

Having had her say, she gratefully took the offered seat, but bristled under the hypocrisy of this man's feigned concern. "Save your sympathy. Of course it hurts. Did you think that it wouldn't? Did you bring me here to taunt me, to bait me with your concern? What do you want from me?" Her directness was likewise noted, if not appreciated. Luther shifted around for a moment, and decided to answer in kind. She obviously remembered nothing of her attack and was equally puzzled by it. They could discover together.

"Do you remember how you were hurt?"

She looked around. No face revealed how to respond. They were blank and inquisitive, and her secret belief that they were responsible, that someone of these people had inflicted the wound out of hate or revenge, began to waver. "No."

Luther nodded to Kai. "Tell her." The young man looked down, summoned the words he had been preparing for three days, and breathed deeply.

"You were shot by one of your own weapons, one of your own people."

She was stunned. It took a moment to sink in. "I thought that . . ."

"That we had done it? That would not make sense. Besides, we aren't like that."

She stared back at the old man. Of course it would not make sense. That had nagged her thoughts as she tried half-heartedly to understand the why of her wound, and accepting instead the easy logic of an either/or answer: enemies kill, friends do not. She had not faced the alternative possibility, although it was obvious that if Kai's people wanted her dead, she would be dead. But one of her own?

"We cannot understand either. Why would one of your own people try to kill you, and why . . ." but Luther hesitated, caught between two urges. He looked to Kai.

Kai swallowed hard. "And why would Lorn be the one to do it?"

Her eyes were wild in disbelief as she looked to Kai. Her face drained of color. She looked from one to another, and then to the ceiling, then the fire as the hint of tears came to her eyes. "Where is he? I must . . . I must . . ." Kai would not let her go on.

"He is dead. I killed him before he could finish his task. He hesitated, and I killed him." He didn't go on. He didn't offer what he believed would explain the small raiding party, its obvious differences with the parties of the past. The silence grew intense, but Luther did not want to lose the momentum.

"Bring in the others." Three of the raiders came through

the door, single file, each guarded by two men. They were dressed as Kai's people, and had their hands tied, even the one with a broken leg who leaned upon a guard for support.

Ursla looked from one to another, their faces revealing everything before her cold gaze. There was no need for words. She began to suspect. However, one captive could not bear her silence.

"But Director. You know the rule. No one is to be taken captive."

She laughed at him. It was a bitter laugh, chilling in its sudden loudness and so out of place. Besides it, her only response came with her hands, which swept around the raiders, revealing their very own situation, their own bonds.

"Take them back to their rooms." Luther waited to continue. He had seen enough to convince him how he must proceed. "So, daughter, you asked for honest answers. Do we get the same in return?" There was a dull, tired look on her face that revealed, if not resignation, at least compromise.

"Yes. The same. But we understand each other, don't we?"

"Perhaps. We will see. But first, why did your father try to kill you?"

She shifted restlessly, the pain apparent, and not solely physical. The reserve was cracking. "I can only guess. There is the rule, of course, but I suppose it was only a justification. Since they are all men, I assume that they had other motives. They might want to change how our system works. I have no way of guessing how things now stand, back there, but things may have changed a great deal when Kai turned out the lights and carried me away. Most of my people have never faced such a thing, such a threat." She looked at him, but not by way of accusation as much as with a sudden revelation about the odd ways the future comes into being.

"And what else do you suspect?"

She looked back at Luther at a loss to answer. "What do you mean?"

"You have a rule against being taken captive. From what Kai tells us it may not be a very good rule, but I can understand why you would have it. If one is taken, she might reveal too much—who your people are, where they are—but Lorn did not try to kill his comrades when they were taken, only you. Perhaps he wanted to become the leader, instead of you. Perhaps he saw his chance. Only you who knew him can best say. However, there is another possibility. Perhaps he was frightened by what only you could reveal, and what the others could not."

She began to develop a respect for this old man. His powers of deduction were sharp, like Kai's. "Perhaps."

Luther smiled, but only on the outside. "I see." And now he began to fidget. What would come of these next few moments? What future would be determined by their words? A great deal—maybe everything—depended upon how she would react as they talked, as revelations came, and on how much she actually knew. She could pose a threat, or even a hope for salvation, and only her reactions would determine the fate of his people, and hers, as the moment approached. But they will also determine her own, immediate future, he thought. She might live; she might die. Luther felt his age grow heavy upon him.

"Come, daughter, the time for reserve is over. It is time to share what we know. Kai has told us of your world. We know you are aware of our past, of our shared ancestors, but how much more do you know? Why did we fight? Why are there so many differences between us?"

She looked around her. How far could she go? How much could she reveal to these people, and what was happening back there, in the mountain? "Your people rebelled. They tried to destroy our world, our city. I guess that, like my father, they wanted power."

Luther laughed. It was a sound of pure release, but he saw her discomfort. She had pride, and could be angered or hurt. "I am sorry, but have you quit keeping your precious records? Your people used to be such good records keepers."

She bristled at that. "And that is why so many records were destroyed or stolen during the fighting? You envied our record keeping?"

It was Luther's turn to bristle. How much did she truly know, and how much was speculation? He became tense, gauging the minute effects of his words upon her. Around him, all the men scrutinized her equally well. Kai waited, holding his tongue and sensing the importance of the moment.

"We were not against records, themselves, but the lifeway they contained. Your people grew cold and uncaring. The machines that they used to control this world were more important than the people who built them. Worse, they removed themselves from it and the consequences of their actions." He did not take it the obvious step further, not yet. "They threatened all our lives, the destruction of this world. We, however, argued for another way. At first, we seemed successful. We created villages outside. We tended to our lives and our world. We worked with it, daily and personally. Then, your people started to take advantage. They withdrew into the mountain and began to guard the records and machines and limit our use of them, and they kept us away from making decisions that would affect us all. That could not be allowed."

Her wonder revealed her ignorance, as did her words. "But that was long ago. We need to think of now."

Luther nodded, then continued. "You are right, more right than you know. We need to think of tomorrow. But for that, we need to know the past, and I see your knowledge does not go back far enough, to before the fighting and the division. Perhaps your father knew. That would explain a great deal about his actions, but we will never know, unfortunately. But first, before we talk further, you need to know how crucial our talk is, how important our actions now are." Always the orator, Luther let his words sink in before he cleared his throat and looked her directly in the eye.

"Our world is on the brink of destruction. The signs are here, and the time of change is at hand. We have a sickness that takes our people without remedy. It took Kai's father, as you well know, and your people have it too. We have waited for it to come, and now it is here, but there is hope." He paused once again for emphasis.

"This man has had a vision, and you were in it. If we read this vision correctly, and we believe we do, you two are both the future and the culmination of another vision from the distant past, an attempt to save and survive and make a better life. We shall see. Can you read?"

197

She nodded, muttering "Of course."

"Good. Then you will read one of the records from long ago, one we saved from the fighting. You will read it aloud to Kai, who has not been taught to read yet but who must understand what and who we are. One day, he might have kept this record himself, and used it to make important decisions. Now . . . before you go, I will reveal one fact for you since the thing you read is only a fragment, a surviving piece of something longer called The Chronicle." He paused. Almost as if by command, everyone shifted in their places, everyone except Ursla. She was fastened to his words, his eyes.

So, some things did remain from the past. Her hope began to rise. Perhaps, no matter how things stood back in the mountain, she could return with this record and once more be an unchallenged Director. The Council would obviously be impressed. They had suspected, but never known for certain. On the raids, they had made quick searches, but found nothing, no records. The old man cleared his throat again to begin.

"This world is on the verge of destruction, because of our ancestors. They made it. They brought it into being with their knowledge and their machines. Everything—the trees, the daylight, the animals—are the result of their purpose. You will understand, as you read, what that purpose was. The time is here for it to be realized, or lost, but we are not sure how to fulfill our part. That is up to you, because your people and ours must act together, or we will all surely die together."

Luther nodded to a man to his left who rose and left the

room. He then leaned toward Kai and asked him to get drinks, and, when they arrived, the atmosphere, the mood, in the room changed. A low murmur developed among the men, and Ursla visually relaxed. It was as if by consensus they had all agreed that they must take a communal breath, a small respite before their next great exertion.

Ursla's shoulder and neck still ached and although her heart was heavy with thoughts of Lorn, she recognized her incapacity to change the past, but also her power to affect the future. For now, she sank into a moment of inaction. For now, she would heal, and then she would act. Kai watched her closely, and was rewarded with a tentative smile, warm but cautious. Although at a loss to explain or understand all he had heard, he, too, was content to wait.

The man returned. In his extended hands he carried something rectangular wrapped in leather that had marks and symbols burned into its surface. This was placed beside Luther, who paused to look around the fire and wait for order and silence to return. Then, carefully, he placed the thing in his lap. His hands rested on it lightly, palms down, as his eyes half closed. He took an audible deep breath. The recitation began.

"The Chronicle was born with this world. It tells of the beginning. Out of a barren and lifeless void, came life and generations. Into the darkness, came light. It is only part of what was, these words written by a man from that time, but it is enough to help us to understand." His eyes opened wider as he looked down and drew a small string that held the leather in place. He unwrapped it, and in the glow from the flickering fire and growing darkness, Kai could see the cold, smooth, metallic surface. He leaned closer, as did Ursla beside him. The light danced on the dark metal.

"The Chronicle tells of strife and war, of the loss of freedom, respect and hope. But it also tells of human integrity and self-sacrifice, and the desire to survive, to keep human blood flowing in human veins." He looked back down and removed a small, pointed sliver from his robe. To Kai, it appeared to be bone. With this, Luther pricked his own finger, and squeezed it until a dark red drop appeared. It, too, reflected the light, even as the old man leaned forward to place it on the object on his lap. Although Kai stretched, he could not see where, nor understand why, but immediately the thing came to life, whirring into a low hum that slingshot Kai back to the city in the mountain, the only place he had ever heard a similar sound.

"A genetic lock!" All the men turned to Ursla. Luther smiled at her before he, too, returned his attention to The Chronicle, which now began to make a louder noise, and then came a sharp click. Its depth began to expand quickly, but stopped half again its previous size. Kai suddenly realized that it was a container, and inside he could see lighter material, stacks of it.

"This record was damaged during the fighting between our ancestors. It was kept in one of the villages on the far side of the mountains. At one time, there were five villages over there, and five on this side. Now, only four remain on this island of life surrounded by the barrenness of our world. But here we have had food enough to survive, until recently, and we have been able to live peaceful, caring lives, until now.

The Chronicle will explain many of the reasons for this, but it will also raise many questions, as it has for us all. It will also show you why we are so concerned by what has happened recently. Of all the villages, ours is the only one to possess such a record, unfortunately. All others have been lost. All the crucial ones that answered the important questions, of how to survive the catastrophe that awaits us. Perhaps, though, once this woman understands our fears, she can help us overcome them. Maybe, our answers are in her city. We shall see."

He handed The Chronicle to Kai. "Keep it opened, and read it only here, tonight. Do not let it out of your sight. If you grow tired, call me. I will close it and place it in safe-keeping and open it again tomorrow, after you rest. Now, I will rest, and return in a while."

He accepted the container, but as Luther slowly rose, Kai was overwhelmed by the stark memory of the night of his first initiation, and of the attack. It came back in a flood so powerful that it swept him helplessly before it: the fire, dream, collapse and struggle to get outside. The avalanche, the flickering fire beyond. He began to sweat and feel the hunger and weariness he felt then. Luther noticed this and mistook it for a reaction to the heavy demands put on a man so young. "What is the matter?"

"I don't know. I guess so much has happened in so short a time."

"Go easy. Take your time. More surprises await you. Take them slowly, one at a time. If it becomes too much, let me know. We have enough time to wait, for a while." His uncle withdrew from the room, followed by the others.

Kai looked at the thing, now resting in his own lap. It was odd. He felt its smooth, hard surface. Absentmindedly, his fingers began to explore its edges. His mind began to open to it. His awareness grew warm.

Chapter Twelve
# Ghosts Speak

Who are you? And when you are. What do you do to pass your days as you spin through space on our little world? Do you live well? Do you love, hate?

I would honestly like to know. I would, in all honesty, like to know because I will never see you or hear you or . . .? But I am the one stuck with the task of writing this all down. I'm the only one of our team who's written anything other than tech reports. This is an old way to communicate that I learned when I was young from reading books in school and at home, so I have been told to write this on these sheets of paper, but who am I writing it for? Someone I don't know and someone who may be very different from me, someone I may not even be able to imagine.

But write I must, perhaps only for me, so that I can understand better and feel good about what we're doing. Or, for my oblivion, possibly only for my executioner. If the wrong people get ahold of this, we're all dead. No way to anticipate either, no way to know if I am reaching one, and not wanting to reach the other, so I simply write, as it is.

We are in the third generation of rule by The Committee. For that long it has had complete power in all things—at first only public things, but now private things too—and our lives have been perfectly safe and secure. There has been no war, as in my ancestors' days when war was a fact of life. There is no crime, except us I guess. The social reasons for humans hurting humans have been controlled. The escalation of crime, which threatened to bring my grandfather's generation to chaos, is no more. We can walk at night without fear. And we all have work to do.

Does that sound good to you? Do you need security, safety, a way to make a living? Then listen, and learn. Our ancestors needed these things, too. They desired them so much it became an obsession. The Committee was created out of this obsession.

It grew from circumstances. It grew through circumstances. And then it became circumstances. In one spark of time our world—a world of great variety, of many peoples and lifeways, each with its own marvelous way of governing and surviving—was lost. The first global ecological (should I say economical?) riots blasted our world into smaller and more manageable chunks as those who had wealth and ease protected what they thought was theirs. Nations fell and small communities fought one another.

Then, the need to protect ourselves became the priority and technology offered us ways to do it. It bred better ways of travel and communication. It was only inevitable that those in power would see the future potential as the threat of global collapse came with the first starvation wars, when those who had nothing but poverty and fear were turned against one another. Those who had neither poverty nor fear, but who developed a plan to keep us busy aided them in their fight. But they did not consider well enough. They misunderstood the people. They didn't know us.

Kai stopped her. "I don't understand. Who is this talking?" She shook her head without looking up from the thing in her hands.

"I don't now. Some type of record, but who wrote it, and why? And look. Parts of it are missing. See the seared edge? And pages are damaged. I can't read this one, or this one either. It picks up again here."

So we have decided to leave, now that the chance has presented itself. The chance for the irony is too great to pass up. Some of us have applied for transfer to The Project, to monitor our work more closely, we said on our applications. But also because we have discovered why The Committee has pushed to get this thing done.

It began innocently enough. At first, the idea of the reclamation of one moon seemed logical, once it was theoretically possible. I don't know. If you're reading this, some part of our work is alive. Maybe it means nothing to you, but. . . you must understand how we are, or were.

Think of it. For the first time in the history of our species, to be able to bring a barren, lifeless thing—this moon—to life! And we can do it. We knew we could pull it off. For many of us, it was the opportunity to prove our theories, to use our technology in life giving ways. This was the chance to realize, in our lifetimes, long years of work and struggle, to see our ideas take shape, form and application. It was everything. So, they sought us out, one by one.

I did research in electromagnetic fields, another did research in fusion, others in gravitation, astrophysics, botany. We had made our discoveries. We knew how our sun works. We had the technology. They used it.

It didn't take long to find the motivations behind the money we were given to do our research. The Committee is not noted for its spending on projects solely for knowledge or the good that can come from them. That's how they kept their power, by monitoring us with the technology scientists provided, by controlling our lives with the communication and surveillance networks that we built.

Once we began working with the idea of colonizing, of sending people up to make the moon livable, we realized that the project had another purpose. First, we thought they would send people there to relieve the population on our own world. Then, we thought that it might become a prison. But, finally, we understood. They intended the moon for themselves. From there, they would have complete control with no threat from the population: systematic and complete surveillance of our world through SATSCAN. As they sit beyond reach and reproach, they would manipulate and we would be even more powerless to stop them.

It is ironic, isn't it? That their own secret plot for control could be used against them and turned into our means of escape, our way to survival? And now I've said it. If this falls into the wrong hands—the threat of any record—I am a dead woman, and so is our plan.

We intend to steal the moon! Crazy, isn't it? We're going to take The Project right out from under their noses, saving ourselves and maybe our race. It will not be easy, but several groups of us have planned it carefully, over three years now, and the figures and projections have been plotted and re-figured, checked and rechecked. We're right. It can be done. We can send this lump of matter off into space, out of our system and into the void. Later, much later, it will spin near another world, a place fit for our race. If our devices work well, if they can withstand the wear of time, if our gravity-controlling sun can survive in the void, we may just . . .

Kai shook his head, half rising from his place near the fire. His hands came up, palms upward in a universal, non-verbal gesture of ignorance and frustration. There was movement behind him and he turned into his uncle's frown.

"That is all that remains." Kai shook with the slightest of tremors as Luther's words shattered the night. "It was badly burnt and scorched. That is all we could salvage."

And then there was only silence punctuated by the sounds of the dwindling fire that drew Kai's eyes and full attention. Ursla stared into its comfort as well. They both had expected a longer explanation. This was so brief, hardly a chronicle at all, but as they lulled in the dance of the flames, it began to grow.

Outside, dawn approached and the silence of the slumbering village was slowly pierced by the early morning songs of birds, sharp and shrill and quickly mounting as the sun rose in the east.

Their minds could not grasp or encompass even a small number of the implications of the little they had learned. Instead, they became animated by brief glimpses and chunks of connections that all mounted into the shape of a question.

"But, it is our world. It is everything. Is it what The Chronicle says, something made for a journey? Did they succeed?" Kai looked to his uncle, his eyes full of disbelief, but also wonder. "Are we there yet? Where are we?"

"No, we are still traveling. This is the world she is describing. Ursla can probably better explain it. I know nothing of how this was done. Over the years my father, and his father, and I have only been able to decipher bits. Put together with the things that have been handed down by word of mouth only, this is what we have concluded." He paused to look again into Ursla's eyes, seeking the slightest clue of guile or deception. There was none, so he began his speculation, moving into knowledge he could not command.

"Our world was once connected somehow to another. This, our world, was barren, just as much of it is still barren today. Except for the villages and their few forests, it is sand and ash, and this was not caused by war." He let the hidden allusion to his vision sink into his nephew's awareness, and then moved on. "As The Chronicle says, our ancestors brought all living things here. Somehow, they made them grow and reproduce, and they made rain and, of course, the sun."

As if by signal, all three looked to the growing patch of light in the window. It had been a common, mundane thing. Now it was filled with wonder, mystery, and awe.

"Of course! They did it in the city in the mountains too. It's only bigger."

"Exactly. That is what I thought when you told us about it."

They both turned to Ursla, completely silent since she stopped reading. Her mind was racing, bouncing from one thing to another. Her world was crumbling into chaos, and she could not hold it together.

"We're doomed then."

Kai was momentarily shocked from his wonder by the ominous resignation coloring her tone, and then he, too, remembered Luther's warnings.

His uncle's voice startled him. "I had hoped you would see a way." Kai looked from one to the other. "Your people don't know how?" Kai was getting lost, and this was too important to lose. He needed to understand.

"What are you two talking about? What do you mean 'How'?"

Ursla could not drop her stare from Luther's pleading eyes. "The Chronicle tells us why. Our ancestors created this world for a group of people called The Committee, but then they stole it. They sent it spinning off into space with its artificial sun and atmosphere, and its passengers. It is self-contained, and it is going somewhere, but we don't know where, or when it is to get there. More importantly, we do not know what to do when it does. We don't know how to stop it, how to get it to do the things it would need to do when we get to where we are going." As Kai listened, the words became jumbled, the reasoning convoluted and frightening.

"Can't we just keep on going, forever? Now that we know of each other, things will be better. Our people will work together now." Luther shrugged, but Ursla became even more agitated.

"The Chronicle says that they had plotted a course. That means that when we get to the world it mentions, their computations end. That was their only goal. We do not know what is beyond it, and none of my people could possibly tell us. We can make simple computations and projections, but not about what is out there in the void and beyond." She gestured upward. Neither man followed her upturned fingers. "Too much has been lost to do more than maintaining the machines." She stopped short and looked to Luther. "So, that was the cause of the split, and the fighting. Your people hated the machines. They wanted to go backwards."

He shrugged. "I only know what has been handed down to me, and it tells me nothing about 'backwards'."

"But they destroyed the records. Didn't they know they were destroying themselves, too? Their world and their descendants?"

"I'm not sure who knew about all of this by the time the split occurred. I do know that they did not want to destroy the world and the future. That is why every effort was made to safeguard some important things, the things that would be needed, then discarded, once we reached our destination." Then he paused. He took a deep breath, and as the air came into him he decided to finish it and let her respond as she would. Then he would know her by the ways she reacted.

"But that is only part of the reason they fought. Some people wanted to make sure something like The Committee would not happen again, and they saw the machines as a threat of this happening. And another, smaller group of the first people decided that this world would become too small. It is said that more people came to it than was planned. Too many, for so little space. Some moved outside, before the world was ready, those who wanted to help the world grow to feed and support more people. Some of those inside, a small secret group, had another idea. They wanted the world as it was to support only a certain number of people. They started to experiment. They created a disease . . ."

"No! That's impossible. Don't blame it on my people. I'm the Director. I would know if it had been . . ."

"But this was long ago. Besides, how long has the disease been with us? Not long. In our villages over thirty people have died, or are dying." He looked compassionately to Kai, whose gaze had dropped to the floor. "How many have died in your city?" He did not wait for an answer. "You see? My ancestors were the first infected. We were outside. We were a threat to the stability of the community as a whole. Yet we saw what was happening. We saw it in their eyes and in their hearts." Kai's growing alarm was apparent. "Relax nephew. We know little about the disease. The laboratory where it was made was destroyed when the people rose up in revolt. Unfortunately, in the fighting all the records were destroyed as well. But, ultimately, it makes little difference. They knew of no cure. That was the point, you see, but with records, perhaps . . ."

"I don't understand. Uncle, no cure? A disease, but what is it? Why?"

"To control population—the number of people. It is deep, deep within our bodies, our very being. When the numbers grow too large and the supplies and resources can't support us, when the stress of numbers comes, the disease comes as well. It attacks our blood. People die. Equilibrium, a balance is maintained."

They all fell silent, pondering the dismal aspects. "But why do we not grow more food, make more resources?"

"A good idea, but we are enclosed here. There is a limit, even if we knew how to make sand and ash productive, or what would happen to everything else if we did that. If you add one thing here, what effect does it have somewhere else? The ones who made this world also created that balance, so if it's upset, what are the effects on us? Besides, how do you make something out of nothing? We have tried as best we could. We tried to expand the forests and fields, early on after the war, but it seems that it cannot be rushed. It is so complex, this growing and expanding, that we had very little effect. And sometimes we did harm trying to do right."

"And in the city, we strictly control births, but even that is not enough. We didn't know about the disease. We didn't know it is tied to population." She looked to Luther with an accusing stare.

"Daughter, don't blame us for your self-imposed isolation. At first, that was the idea of the secret group. But later, you chose to raid our villages and kill our loved ones, so don't blame us for your ignorance."

"But we did it because of the disease. We thought we needed new blood and new leaders with your intuitive abilities. We didn't know that . . ."

Luther nodded his head while he stared respectfully at the floor. "You took women, and women here do not know the history of our troubles. We men have kept it secret, for good reasons. Life is full of these sad ironies."

Their silence lengthened and Luther was beginning to wonder if he should stir and get some food. It was time, but his appetite was less that hearty. He ate little as the years accumulated, but this reflection was shattered by his nephew's voice.

"We have two problems: the disease and the world's journey." It sounded so simple, even as he said it. "Perhaps we could defeat the disease, if we kept our numbers down and as the forests stretched out into the waste. Maybe not. Sooner or later, even with the whole world covered, we would have more people and more problems trying to control our numbers."

"Yes, that's what the others saw, and that is why they created the disease. Sadly, we have never written these things down. We learned our lesson about records. They can be used for evil, selfish purposes, to control and rule. Besides, if this story of our world were to become common knowledge there would be fighting and fragmentation as small groups moved off to isolate themselves and hoard resources. That is not what we should become. Also, this heavy burden gives our people a center, a group that knows this awful truth and must look out for all." He looked to Ursla. "Perhaps your people have one, too. Perhaps Lorn was their leader."

She was frozen by the thought. As its chill sank in it provided the last blow to her reserve and she saw the terrible, painful logic. It explained a great deal.

Luther did not push the matter, but tried instead to redirect their efforts. "The disease does not worry me as much as the other." He let them think and focus on this problem, then continued.

"Yes. The disease could be defeated, for a long time, perhaps forever, if we could only solve the other. However, as Ursla says, we do not know what waits beyond that one place our ancestors chose as our destination. It is unknown, I think. I mean, what if we have already passed this place?" The thought was not his alone. They each had felt it lurking in the background and each had refused to bring it out for discussion, but it could not be ignored. This was a possibility, and they were dealing in many possibilities. "It is unknown, and we must work in certainties."

Kai thought back to his own journey into the frightening unknown. Reality was one thing, the fear it generated another. To deal with the former, one needed to ignore the fear. If one perished, if all perished, one could feel satisfied in knowing actions were well intended—deliberate and carefully planned—and therefore appropriate. "We must try to fulfill our ancestors' dream. We must prepare to go to a new world, when the time is right. The preparation is important. It may be everything."

"That's easily said, Kai, but we don't know when. And even if we were not concerned about that and simply waited for it to happen, we would still have to know how. How do we make the move? You don't simply pack your things and walk there. You don't merely sprout wings and fly into the sun!" His raised eyebrows stopped her. Then, she smiled. "O.K. You do, but getting to another world is quite a different thing. I have no idea how they planned to do it. I have no idea how they got here. We just do not know. None of my people has this knowledge." The sense of hopelessness that filled the room was palatable. However, Kai would not be deterred.

"But the people on the world we came from must know how to do it. What did The Chronicle say? That the rulers would rule from here? They must have been able to talk between worlds. Perhaps . . ."

Luther could not respond quickly enough. Ursla was so attuned to Kai's reasoning that she had half-formed the question herself, then spoke it aloud without realizing it.

"Perhaps. We have communication devices. We use them to keep in touch with our people outside the city. They always seemed too powerful for such a limited purpose. Perhaps we could . . ."

"There is no one to contact." They both turned to Luther simultaneously. He looked to Kai first. "Do you remember the fire, the night of your initiation?" He felt very odd, mentioning this private, secret thing in front of a stranger, an outsider, and he went no further with it, confident in his nephew's ability to comprehend. For Ursla, he formed a simple pronouncement. "There is no one to contact, back there. Although we do not know the extent of the destruction, there was a major catastrophe. Some believe our ancestors created it. When they removed this moon, they may have upset the delicate balance of the world they left behind. However, I believe they destroyed themselves; that war came when The Committee found itself trapped on a world it had hoped to dominate from here. The cause may not be important now. If anyone survived, they could not help us. They have their own lives and survival to attend to. If . . ."

She did not question his facts, for facts they were as surely as if she had known them all along. And she felt no real sense of loss because these were not real beings to her, only the sounds of words from an old man's mouth.

Kai, however, felt them personally. He had seen it, the end in flames. The mother and child, so long dead.

For Luther, the pain was sharp and acute. It lived beyond a level of the mind. It came from the deep place inside, somewhere near his backbone, and he knew it to be true because of this. Because of the pain, he had become a leader, because he cared, without making demands or asking for relief. Even if these people were long dead, they would not be forgotten. They would still be mourned, because they once were humans and that counted for something or all else was insignificant. For all three sitting quietly before the dead fire, the sense of isolation and loneliness was intense.

"So much has been lost." Kai and Luther agreed with slow, thoughtful nods. "How? How did they accomplish this marvelous thing? Create it all and send it off? If only The Chronicle had not been partially destroyed." Her despair grew upon the others. Luther, however, had been through it all before, many times, in his head.

"Daughter, The Chronicle would not tell us how. It was only to tell why they did it. There were other records that went with it. They told what was to be done when we arrived at the end of the journey. I had hoped that your people had them. Mine do not any longer. During the fighting, they were kept separate so that if one were lost, others might survive. Things were so chaotic then. We moved about, here then there, to hide. To fight. I was told by my father that one of my ancestors, was the keeper of the last record. When he moved us into this village, he brought it with him. He was killed, and the record was not found with him, so it was assumed that your people had captured it again. Too much has been lost through time, down the generations. So much forgotten, so much lost. It was only one more thing, but one crucial thing."

The voice inside Kai was screaming. "But uncle, it may not be lost."

Everyone, all the elders, wanted to help, but it was too early to attract attention to their doings, and their reasons. They would tell the villagers when the time came so that they could prepare. For the moment, secrets had to be kept to avoid panic, and to keep the people together and working as a group. But, despite their restraint, all the elders were excited, young again in their sense of discovery, purpose, and hope. It was decided that only Kai, Luther and one other should go. They sent for Shawn, who was strong and respectful enough to keep his silence.

With Luther outside as a guard at the ruin of the holy place, the two friends squeezed through the narrow hole pushing their digging tools ahead of them. Even with two of them working, the going was very slow, and made even more so by Luther who interrupted their work repeatedly for reports of their progress. At last, using one tool as a lever, Shawn gave a desperate heave and Kai tugged the rectangular box out through the crack between the two wall stones of the doorframe. It was, as he had guessed, a record. Shawn's surprise was obvious, and he grew excited, but he held his tongue.

Outside again, Kai handed it to his uncle, whose eyes brimmed with tears. It was too early to tell, but at least there was hope for now. As odd and impossible as it seemed, there was hope.

The thing rested on a low table near the fire in Luther's home. The three had now been joined by all the elders, so many eyes tried to devour it where it rested. There was only one obvious thing to do, but Luther hesitated, wishing instead to hold this one moment of potential, but then, prolonging it may be damaging too, he thought. If it is not the record they needed, the disappointment may be damaging if the anticipation were allowed to build too long.

So, he stepped to the table, withdrew the sliver, and pricked his finger. The drop of blood fit into the shallow indentation on one side, and as Kai watched, it spread out to fill the tiny basin, and then disappeared. Before he could wonder how metal could absorb liquid, the thing began to hum, then came an audible whir and click as it popped open.

There was a collective sigh from the group, and spirits rose because no matter what the thing contained, it had been keyed to Luther's genetic code. It had belonged to his ancestors, and this was indeed a good sign.

However, although the thing seemed intact, its contents were useless—incomprehensible, indecipherable—to the group. As Luther gingerly thumbed through it looking for a common point of reference, Ursla looked over his arm. "But this must be it! At least it is a technical manual. I can recognize some of it, and look here . . ." She stepped in front of Luther, taking up his search with her own hands as if by signal. "These are programming notes—instructions for the computers." She continued to scan through it, stopping periodically to take a closer look at a page or a diagram. Seconds collapsed together into long moments of silence that seemed to be punctuated only by her quickened breathing. The instant of anticipation grew heavy and difficult.

She finally looked up into the expectant faces surrounding her. Noon had passed, and the sun's rays slanted through the opposite windows showing dust motes swirling through their tiny universes. The shadows had begun to lengthen.

"This must be it, or at least part of it. First, it's keyed to Luther. Next, it's full of long and intricate computer instructions, which are interrupted twice with charts. Look." Their eyes dropped dutifully to the record. Groups of variously sized circles spotted the page. Beside each were numbers and figures. She flipped several pages together, and another appeared, similar in design and shape to the previous one, but subtly different in the placement of the circles. Their relative sizes remained unchanged; only their positions had changed. As if by signal, they all looked back to her, to each other, and to Luther. As their attention lowered again to the record, Kai put their thoughts into words.

"But what does it all mean? Charts of what?"

She hesitated before she answered. After all, her knowledge was limited, but there were clues in the records she was familiar with and there had been debates among her people, scholarly arguments citing past beliefs and conjectures. Her silence made those ideas stir. She walked around the table and the slight wind currents this sudden movement generated sent the motes spinning off in unanticipated directions.

"I'm not a technician, so my knowledge isn't of these things, and my people don't have someone whose job it is to understand the universe around our world, but there has always been discussion about it. There are the night constellations, and we have people who watch them closely, trying to unlock their mysteries. But it is mostly a game with them, a puzzle, and they are not too serious so little has been discovered, and even less understood. Now, after spending time here with you and hearing of our shared past—of our old world from The Chronicle—then I think these charts are of other worlds, perhaps some like our own, and I assume that one of them is our destination, the one our ancestors saw as our new beginning."

There was a loud murmur of approval, and then as it dawned upon them that the very salvation of their people may be at hand, the murmur grew louder and more jovial. It was the spontaneity of relief, a release of pent-up anxiety that had come to dictate their lives and to direct their actions for the bulk of their adulthood, but now, as suddenly and easily as this, it had come to an end.

Only Kai and Luther remained unmoved, and although they stood on opposite sides of the table, their focal point was the same: the jumble of numbers and figures and letters on the page of the record before them. Gradually, all the others' attention drew back also to the same point. Their reserve was easily understood, and grudgingly appreciated.

Luther looked around at the faces he had known so long and so well. Together, they had decided so much for their people, and wondered about so much. Together, they had joined in their people's love of one another and it had always seemed so right, so indomitable, and he had satisfaction in the belief that his ancestors had made the correct choice, that their movement outside the stale and limited confines of the mountain city had been the right thing to do, and that their emphasis on community had reaped all the benefits they desired. But now, generations later, it may have come to nothing. Now, their descendants were in great danger, and they could not remove that danger.

Ursla and Kai had been studying aspects of the same dilemma, but, understandably, from very different points of view, yet they reached the same conclusion almost simultaneously, although for Kai it came as an act of faith—a belief in the power and meaning of his vision—and for Ursla an act of logic. "I must return to my people, with this and The Chronicle."

"And I must return with her."

Luther braced for a wave of objections, quite possibly a long and heated debate, but there was neither. Their only course was obvious, once it was voiced by the two people the group had already accepted as the shapers of their future. After all, they could not understand the record, but her people might. Neither record could be used against them now, but only for the rescue of their doomed world. Later, if there was a later after this moment and the overriding problem had been resolved, they could talk with her people, show them their way of life, talk about what was important, and perhaps even in this time of great change, something good could be salvaged. For the moment, their task was simple: wait, have faith, and hope.

"Tonight, we will feast for these two young people, to send them on their way with full bellies and spirits lightened by our gathering. So, go and prepare. Tonight we celebrate. Tomorrow, we discuss how to tell our people about what happened so long ago, and what is to come."

The first day they did not speak to one another. They merely communicated the few necessary things with facial expressions—a question about being ready to move on, one about the need to rest. For Kai, this was partially the result of his uneasiness about what to expect, both on the trail and above. At the last moment of their departure, and without coaxing, he had set aside the weapon he had resolved to carry. Instead, he took his spare bow, to get food he rationalized, but also, just in case. They had no way of knowing how Ursla's people would respond upon her return, but he concluded it would be best to show a peaceful intent at least, and rely on his vision. For the time being, the prisoners remained in the village, and the guards on the trail.

For the first day and night, they did not speak. Kai simply stepped off in the lead, and Ursla followed, wrapped in her own thoughts and anxieties. That evening, he slowed and then motioned her off the trail, where he built a fire and she rummaged through her small sack of food. They ate in silence, staring into the flames lost in images of the past, longings for a future. As she stretched out to sleep, warmed by the fire and the tasty food she had grown accustomed to savoring, she began to thaw.

The evening before, at the feast, she had felt for the first time a glowing sense of belonging. As the people laughed and joked with one another, as children ran about lost in their own world and games, as individuals periodically fell silent after dinner and looked benignly around them and up to the night lights, a dull, beaming calm and satisfaction so evident on their faces, she began to realize how happy and full their lives really were.

She softened; she changed. Her world had always been two-halved, like a switch. Things were either this way, or that. Outside, inside. Night, day. Them, us. Now, she was beginning to appreciate the twilights, the gray hues of dawn. Now, she was also beginning to appreciate this man, sleeping on the far side of the fire from her. His voice startled her, and for a brief second she feared, then hoped, he had read her thoughts and the hard, naked images they had become.

"I've been thinking. There are still too many things I don't understand." The fire crackled. "Like, what are the night lights? As a boy, I imagined them to be small fires, built by sky people to keep them warm at night. Now, I think they may be like our sun. They come out when it is gone. And they are far away. But maybe I was right. It makes more sense for them to warm sky people. People like us."

She looked above her. "There are so many." She realized then that she had very little acquaintance with them, that her trips outside her mountain city had been few over the span of her life, and even then her wonder had never been directed upwards. "There are so many."

"Um, hmm. But more than there used to be it seems. They are always changing. They're never the same. But alike. They come out; they go away."

They were silent a long while, so out of place their voices seemed in the dark, quiet night forest. She decided that he must have fallen asleep, so she wavered in her decision to speak to him, to make peace. They would need to work together, so she resolved to talk to him before they reached the mountain.

When her breathing evened out into an easy, recognizable pattern, Kai cursed himself for being a cowardly fool. To talk of the lights above when other things needed to be said. He had started to say them several times that day, but when he opened his mouth, no words came out. His mind ran around all of these things until it became too tired to go further, and he slept.

All the next morning she walked silently behind him, at first thinking only of what lay ahead. But, as the day warmed, as her blood pumped with the exertion of her thighs growing hot with the steepening trail, as his back side swayed in front of her, flexing under his own exertion and gathering more and more of her attention, she began to forget about the people in the mountain and focus, instead, on the person in front of her.

He could feel her behind him; he could feel the shift in her thoughts, and finally, as the sun reached its peak, he could feel her need to connect, like the heat of the sun on his back.

The small stream waited. When they reached it, he did not hesitate or speak. He removed his clothes and dove into its cool solitude. They spent the afternoon swimming in the shallow pool, and talking of things to come. They drew closer together, and understanding emerged without words. That night, they slept locked together under the night lights, awed by their brightness and proximity. No matter how her people reacted, they were two, but insepa-rable. No matter what their future would be, they would find it, together.

Chapter Thirteen
# The Beginning in the End of the Beginning

They stopped at the base camp below the mountain only long enough to rest and eat a last mid-day meal before the steep, final ascent. For Ursla, it seemed a lifetime—perhaps more—since the night she came down that trail, arms bound behind her, jaw and neck aching from the blow Kai had given her, looking for any means to slow them, or to escape. They had talked about it, and he had explained it clearly and with emotion. She had surprised him, and having no time to think, he had responded naturally, instinctively. He should not be blamed, but he might be, by others. She could not, however, escape the fact that his instinct may have saved them all.

It seemed like a lifetime, and now the unknown was about to be made apparent for all her people. What would their reception be? What would be the reaction to the ancient records they carried with them, their containers carefully tied open? She could only hope. With these chaotic thoughts and a stomach knotted with apprehension, she rose and prepared to leave. Her wound wore heavily upon her again.

Why couldn't they simply, quietly walk off—there, into the forest—and disappear? They could live out their lives quietly, without strife and turmoil. They could let others deal with universal threat and disaster. After all, as individuals she and Kai were unnecessary. Their efforts were insignificant, and might not be of consequence in the long run. But, as quickly as she conceived the possibility, she set it aside as he came up behind her, wrapped his arms around her, and pressed them into one mass. This is why. The voice came into her head as if the person who made it were standing right next to her but it did not frighten her. It calmed her with its certainty. They were not alone, and there was a future to be made for those yet unborn. That future required action, and action required people, and—as she had recently learned—dedication to something larger than herself.

When they moved off to the confrontation, she took the lead and he followed, shooting a look ahead over her shoulder, up the trail occasionally. He had played their booby traps against them. They might have learned something from that. He found no threat, no hazards, but he knew, as surely as he felt the hair tingle on the back of his neck, that they were being watched. Although uncomfortable, he did not feel immediately threatened, so he let his attention wander, keeping that one cautious eye periodically scanning forward.

It was a beautiful day. The stream below made its usual, contented sound, and the deep greens of the forest were broken here and there with the yellows, whites and blues of mountain flowers. It was then, as he slipped into the scene passing about him, that the awesome enormity of his ancestors' accomplishment struck him. To conceive, even to imagine, such a complex, intricate and beautiful thing was wonderful in and of itself, but to bring it into being, to make it happen and to have it work, was incomprehensible. The subtleties, the details, the variables of life against life, from one generation to the next, these were indeed monumental considerations for paltry beings like him. And it worked. This complex world worked. This thought gave him a feeling of immense security, of safety. He stopped. Sensing his halt, she stopped, too, and turned to him, a puzzled look on her face. The voice was loud within him, and she felt it, too. He could see it in her eyes.

The wild look in his own eyes stood in stark contrast to the smile playing upon his lips.

"What?"

"This. This. Look around. The trees. The sun. Everything. Imagine what it took. They would not let this go wrong. There is a way for it all to work out. There has to be. All we need to do is find it."

She let her own eyes take in what he saw. Maybe. But there is no planning for human nature—the difficult variable— no way to anticipate future generations. A different place, a different time, a different people. Who knows? "Maybe. Maybe at least the mechanical things still work, if they still exist. We are a systematic people. That's one thing that may not have changed. If everyone followed the systems over the generations, if nothing was lost when the fighting broke out, if, if, if . . . then, maybe, we'll have the technical smarts to do what must be done. But, what about us, deep inside? I don't know what will happen." She turned and continued up the rise, then stopped again.

"And what if our ancestors were wrong? What if this new place isn't what they thought, or what if it has changed over time? How could they be so certain?" She moved off, Kai close behind her, much less enthusiastic than a moment before.

They stopped at twilight behind the last rock outcropping before the tunnel entrance. Kai surveyed the scene. All was quiet. So perfectly had the entrance been made to blend in with the natural rock, he missed it several times before following the trail carefully with his eyes right to it. Now, with his first good look at it, he saw that it was not a tunnel at all, but a structure fabricated from the same rock-like material as the doorway, placed upon the summit of a ridge and molded somehow into the rocky crags above and behind it. To mold a mountain. It was difficult to imagine. This added to his appreciation, for his people thought in giant terms and accomplished their goals. When nothing stirred after several moments, they decide the bold approach advisable and walked directly up the trail to the entrance, which opened at their approach.

Vivian stood in the opening, flanked by two guards bearing weapons, conspicuously. This alarmed Ursla at first, but the older woman's warm, emotion-filled greeting put her apprehension to rest, and the emotion increased as they turned inside.

The excitement generated by her return was profound and pervasive. As they moved off down the corridor toward the main chamber, people popped from doorways to smile, wave and drop into hasty, animated conversations with one another. Throughout the walk, Vivian turned and smiled, then chattered through useless, insignificant news, her relief at Ursla's homecoming obvious.

In the main chamber, they took transports directly to the Council's rooms. Since their climb up the mountain had been carefully scrutinized for any hint of deception or threat to the Director's life, the Council had ample time to meet, discuss, and prepare. The first interview was brief. Ursla related her story directly and without emotion: the night of Kai's escape, her father's attack and, in condensed version, the meetings with Luther and the elders.

"I will not go into details right this moment. I am tired, and I need to visit the doctor. This record fragment explains itself. After you have read it and talked about it, I will return. . . ." She paused and looked around to Kai. "We will return to answer your questions, but first, let me emphasize one point. Our days of isolation are over, and our days are numbered, unless Kai's people and ours can resolve the mystery of this." She took the second record from Kai as he withdrew it from his pack, and carried it to the long, semi-circular table behind which the Council sat.

"Carn. I suggest you look at this carefully. You are our best technician, and you have studied the heavens. Perhaps you and your staff can decipher it. Call in the supervisors from the computer sections. You will need them." She made preparations to leave.

"But Director. Lorn's attack. Why?"

She turned to the middle of the table and a wizened old

man with shrunken hollows below his eyes. He would have withdrawn the question if he could have, the sincere look of pain it had fostered in her was that apparent and compelling, but she answered without hesitation.

"I believe Lorn and the men with him were members of a secret group, the existence of which predates our own first woman Director. I believe its purpose was to insure our continued isolation, and to work against the people—our people—outside. I believe this group has harmed us greatly, and has, in all probability, contributed to our destruction, that is, if we are destroyed. Only time will tell, and only Carn's efforts can save us. In any event, if this group is still intact after Lorn's death and the capture of the others, and if any of its members are present in this room, take heed. The group has no purpose now. The truth is out, and if you wish to survive, we must all survive." Her eyes swept the length of the table and none of the nine faces turned from her stare.

"I suggest you read the fragment first, now, while all are present, and that you make copies before you place the original in the vault. And I recommend that you make copies of the other as well. I want one copy of each sent to me as soon as they are finished." She did not wait for response but turned and walked out the door, Kai close behind. In the corridor, she instructed the two guards to remain with the documents and protect them wherever they were taken.

As they stepped alone aboard the first transport, Ursla let a great sigh escape as her shoulders sagged and drooped, as if the need to bear some great burden had been removed, leaving one tired woman. He realized then what a terrible and stressful journey this had been for her, how much anxiety and tension had traveled with her. As exhaustion lay hold of her, she began to favor her wounded shoulder. The bandage had come off as they swam in the pool and he had tried to fabricate a new one, but it was a crude affair and did not help much. "You need to see the doctor now."

"We'll go home. I will call her from there." She spoke the destination into the machine and they whirred off in that direction, followed by an occasional greeting shouted here and there as they passed.

The doctor arrived just as she finished her bath. She dressed the wound, sprayed on a bandage, and gave her a sedative to make her sleep soundly.

"It's too bad your people don't have technical abilities with medicine."

Kai looked from the doctor's smug glare to Ursla. "If we did, we would not respect the consequences and tragedy of conflict." The doctor departed without another word.

As Ursla dropped off to sleep, Kai asked if he could visit his sister. She rolled to a console behind a panel in the headboard of the bed and spoke into it. He did not hear the words, but he understood the purpose. She had no sooner finished her message and she was asleep, her face relaxed, dreamy and beautiful. Kai kissed her gently; she stirred. He covered her with a blanket, and then left the room to wait for Nata to arrive.

When she came, she did so with a great deal of reserve and show. She allowed him only a short hug, a tentative peck on the cheek. Later, as they stood awkwardly on the terrace of Ursla's home, the artificial night lights blinked above. Not to be put off, Kai broke the strained silence, the feigned interest in the lights above.

"You have changed. What is it?"

She wavered, and then walked to the edge of the terrace to look down upon the night city with its blinking lights, its geometrical arrangement of streets and parks and buildings. "I like it here. That's all."

"I see that. What happened, the night Lori and I escaped? Where were you?"

"I . . . I just decided not to go. That's all." He could see that this caused her pain, and this made him a bit easier for it possibly meant she felt guilt and covered her denial of family and her people with a veneer of haughtiness. He moved next to her.

"How is mother? She was knocked down when we were taken. And Lori and Lan?"

As he told her of their family he leaned closer until his forearms rested on the rail next to hers, their elbows slightly brushing. She keenly felt even this slight touching and its power of connection, of rejuvenation and support. It brought down the barriers she had built around her. This was a thing she sorely missed from her life in the village. This touching, she knew, drew its power from the sharing it evoked, and she was grateful to him for such an undemonstrative gesture.

"You know Nata, it really doesn't matter if you like this place better. Your family understands." He thought back to his few days here, his own "orientation." Perhaps, with time, its attractions would dull. Besides, this place was not actually a complete lie, even though his mother would probably disagree. She could not possibly comprehend Nata's seemingly easy dismissal of family and people. For the moment, however, the concern for their world and its future made personal problems such as these diminish in size and significance. "Besides, soon our people and these people will be together. The isolation is over."

"What do you mean?"

"I mean that we are all going to come together, our people and these here. No more raids, no more battles on the mountainside. We will work together. You can come and go, as you wish." He did not elaborate to tell her why, or that they had once been the same people. He did not think the history or the reasons very important to her, although he could feel that she wrestled with something big and that she was confused. As the silence lengthened, he moved away, back towards the pool and the couch behind it. In a few moments, she joined him.

"But what's going to happen here? Will things change?"

He didn't know what she was searching for, so he answered as generally as possible, hoping to put her mind at ease. "I imagine it will pretty much stay the same." They looked around, and she seemed relieved. "Does that make you happy?"

"Can you imagine what our mother would say if she saw this place?"

"I think she would find some things interesting."

"No doubt."

"When our uncle comes, he will make a great show of indifference." The image was humorous, in a familiar sort of way, but Nata tensed and turned inside herself. Her leaving was like the closing of a door, and Kai understood. So, that's it, he thought. She has found someone here. He leaned back into the cushion to look at the night lights. That's how life works.

Ursla had wondered about us, about the deep changes. Deep. Superficial. Perhaps they are just points of reference and nothing deeply human ever changes. Maybe we are all concerned only with ourselves, and on the outside we let shallow concerns prevail, until . . . Maybe we're like these lights: some seem brighter, some dimmer, but all the same nonetheless. Illusions. Maybe so, he thought. But they, too, are pulled to one another. He noticed dense concentrations, and then lone lights.

He saw relationships everywhere he looked. Some were obvious; others were invisible until the right time came to reveal them. It all depended on where you stood when you looked for them. Nata stood here, inside this place with its own ways of doing things and she saw the village as dim and dismal—a thing from the past and therefore undesirable by comparison. Perhaps we know so very little, actually. Personally, so very little, but this . . . He reached over and took her hand. It was cold, but it warmed as the two intertwined into one mass, a balance sought between the two. This collective connection was something else.

The days that followed were a blur of intense activity. Repeatedly, Kai and Ursla were asked to the Council chamber for an update and to be questioned. Although the issues involved seemed painfully obvious to Kai, the Council seemed perplexed by the revelations of The Chronicle. Finally, when his patience had worn thin with their questions about seemingly unrelated and irrelevant issues, and after his repeated answers of "I do no know" were poorly received by his inquisitors, he made a proposal.

"Look. I will take you to my village. You can meet with my uncle and the elders, the elders from the other villages. You can have a big meeting and question yourselves to death."

To his surprise, the Council agreed, despite the phrasing, but only four members and their support staff made the trip. The others remained behind to work on the other record, which was beginning to demand more and more people, time and computers. The remaining Council members were to keep in contact and attend the meeting by use of the communicators.

Kai's leave-taking of Ursla was brief, but tender. She had her own duties, and some changes to make in preparation for the disclosure of The Chronicle to her people. As he kissed her goodbye, the transport softly whirred behind him, and as he turned, he found Nata sitting in it. She was dressed as his people dressed, and she smiled briefly, without looking directly at Ursla. As the two moved off, she softly said "Just for a visit." He smiled to himself, and put his arm around her for their trip to the outer passage.

The first meetings lasted a long time. At first, early on, they became heated as past wrongs and differences were aired. More often than not, the distant Council members were the most outspoken and demanding, but the universal threat was too great to all concerned and, as the unfolding of events made apparent, this one common thread forced the disagreements into the background while practical matters became the sole focus of discussion. At last, the party prepared to return to the mountains, leaving a Council member behind with a communicator for each village.

Luther walked into the mountains with his nephew, the remaining group of people who came with the Council members, and the prisoners. It was time for him to see, and to consider. He was old, and his time was near. He felt this in his compulsion to make haste, when haste was not necessary, and to put things in their proper places, as if they might be left behind ill prepared for a future owner.

Their return to the mountain was cause for celebration, with Ursla handling every detail herself. Luther and Kai were warmly received with a feast and, after a night's rest, a tour of the city.

Kai was taken by how easily and casually his uncle accepted it all: the hallways, the city inside a cave, the machinery and people. It was as if he had been here before, and as Kai scrutinized him, he saw at times a slight nod, a hidden smile and he knew, without asking, that the old man had indeed seen it before, whole and in detail in words sent to him by ancestors he never knew, words that painted his imagination into a personal vision of something he had never experienced. The images had lingered in language, in stories that were as much a bond between people as the blood they shared. Luther had seen it before, although he had never been here.

But the old man grew gradually tired of the celebration and politely took Ursla aside to ask about the Council. There were still great matters to discuss and decide. Finding his way around could wait until afterwards.

At first, he took Ursla's reaction as disappointment, and was on the verge of phrasing an apology when she explained. "I had hoped to keep you busy, to give my people more time. They have not finished with the record." Taking Luther by the elbow, she moved off away from the others who had followed on the tour. Kai followed them.

They walked into the large park beside the tall buildings, and as they sat on one of its benches Kai felt again the overpowering weight of all that had happened in his recent past. So much had changed and become complicated since he sat on this very bench with Lorn. At that time, he floundered in his ignorance. Now he floundered in his knowledge, but he also saw patterns and logic in things that he could never have recognized on that first day of discovery. Life, indeed, was an odd odyssey.

"Tell me what is happening. Is there difficulty?" Luther's voice jolted him out of his reverie. "Are your people unable to read our records?"

"They have done a lot in the short time they have had the things." Diplomatically, she didn't state the obvious implication, that if they had been aware of The Chronicle earlier they might have done things differently and sooner. "They fed the data from the record into our computers, and they have run test programs. Everything has worked very well, perfectly in fact, with one exception."

"Which is?"

"They cannot pinpoint our location. I knew when we first talked that this would be a problem, but it may not be critical if we could only find our destination. If we could see where we are in relationship to it, nothing else would matter, but we can't. We have no points of reference. In other words, we don't know where we are, or where we are going because the record takes it for granted that we would have those bits of information. It focuses only on the steps to approach our new world, and on our departure for our new home."

Kai's gloomy composure was swept away immediately by the excitement this news generated. So, it was possible, this departure from their world to the new that had worried him so much. "You mean, they have found how we will get from here to there? Do we grow wings and fly into the sun?"

She chuckled, despite herself, and realized how much she had missed him. She looked forward to the coming night, alone with him away from these worries of so many others.

"Not exactly, but you're not far wrong. I don't know all the intricate details since I'm not trained as a technician, but if you like I could take you to them and they could explain."

"I wouldn't understand them if they were to, so just tell me how, in your own words."

"It seems our exit chambers, the hallways that go outside to the mountain slopes . . ." Her jaw ached slightly with the memory of the night he escaped with her and her hand went automatically to her chin, a movement Kai noticed and smiled at. "It seems these were once transport vehicles from our mother planet to this one. Before there was an atmosphere, they connected with the pressurized chambers that we call our city, and which housed all the mechanisms to bring life to this moon. The systems that operate the chambers are one story below the rooms you saw. The chambers are for people. We knew of these levels, but thought them only for storage and back-up mechanisms in case of failures. There have been none, so we never found the need to open them and explore." But now, this is an emergency, she thought, the ultimate one. "We need only blast away the coverings that were used to make them seem a natural part of the mountain from the outside, and the six chambers can be separated from this world."

"How? What makes them work?"

Again she scrambled to find the words suited to her audience. Would they understand, at least accept without question, the principles behind her people's technology and be satisfied that someone somewhere could work out the details? Would they simply go along for the ride, and not cause undo alarm and delay, should the time arrive?

She chuckled again. "It seems that their traveling machines used gravitational fields. Our ancestors were able to create their own, and to use the fields of other bodies, other worlds. That's how they created our sun and put it in its place. That's how our world was released from its mother world and has avoided destruction, how it has avoided hitting other planets or being pulled into other suns."

By the looks on their faces she knew she had lost them, and that it would take too much time, perhaps a lifetime, to acquaint them with the workings of their universe and the theories about it, and it would require their attention, which was so obviously tentative, more an act of courtesy than true interest. "Let's just say these chambers will float free, and use our new world's attraction to pull them down, easily and gently if we handle it correctly." That seemed to satisfy them for the moment.

"So, what's the problem? We can do it. I told you they must have thought of everything."

"But Kai, we still don't know where we are in relation to that world, so we don't know how close or how far away we are, and that also means that we are not certain that we have not gone past it in our ignorance, or if it will be here to-morrow. We just don't know. And the record's instructions make it clear that things aren't going to happen automatically once we come near our new home. We have to feed our computers, reprogram and convert systems to new tasks. Our computers do not have infinite storage capacities, and it takes a lot to keep this planet going. They were given only what was immediately necessary, with the idea that later, when the time was right, they could be redirected. That's one of the reasons so much emphasis was placed on written records. They are safe back-ups that require no maintenance and cannot be erased."

With the possible exception of Luther, whose interest was recaptured by the implications of safe records, she was losing them again. "The records on astronomy and the people who made them are gone. As I said in the village, we have amateurs who study the stars, but this is way beyond their abilities. Their studies have always been sporadic and questionable. After all, the night lights have always changed as we moved through the void. They wouldn't be able to search the skies and spot one tiny little planet out of all . . ." They were gone.

Her sudden silence brought them back, and Kai, the ever simple, seemed confident. "Just tell us what it is you need."

"A map."

"A what?" He was growing impatient with her again.

"We need a way to tell where we are: if we are close to or going away from this planet. We've diverted all our time and energy for a search through all our computers and fragments of records for any information on its location, but so far, nothing. You see, it doesn't make sense to continue with our preparations until this is understood first. If we've passed it, we need to put our efforts into developing the means to survive on our own, without our ancestors' help, to fighting the disease and finding a new, a different home, maybe. That's why the original choice, the original plan, is our best opportunity, but where is this new world?"

"What's a map?"

He was hopeless. "A chart, like the ones in the record you found but one that shows our relationship to those constellations in it. A 'painting' of the night lights, the stars, around the new world. We don't have one."

Kai and Luther studied this dilemma in silence. For all their lives, and the lives of their people, the stars had been a never-ending series of changes. With a very few exceptions, the stars changed as their tiny world spun on its course through the universe. But Kai was a sensitive being, one who studied what he did not understand, walking around the new-found idea until understanding dawned.

"So it would look like a painting of stars?"

"Yes. Something like that."

"And our ancestors built this whole marvelous world to take us to a new one, and did not leave a map for us? Impossible. Even if they were destroyed in the fighting, there would be others. Don't you think they would want us to see what our new home would be like? To prepare us and to keep us in hope? Look at the trees and streams outside. That is what it will be like once we get there. Why would they prepare a world out of nothing only to make it look only like our old one? No. They would make it new. They would make it like they wanted it to be, like they thought the new one they had chosen for us would look like. They'd imagine standing on that new world and try to prepare us for life there. That's why they would show us the stars, the new stars every night."

He looked up and Ursla's eyes followed his. Her mouth dropped open. She sprang to her feet, looking upward, trying to penetrate the illusory daylight into the darkness beyond it.

"Of course! Of course!"

Kai sat quietly and watched them play. They had not seen him yet, so he leaned back into the comfort of the couch and let the pleasure of their games calm him. He was very tired. It had been a long walk, and now these nagging thoughts were clamoring for his attention. He searched back through his cloudy memory to make those images as clear as if new. His father, eyes alive and happy. His mother, her arm broken by the raiders and the joy at their return from the mountains. He thought of leave-takings, but of a different kind, with a departure always implying a return. And now this. A departure without hope of return.

Kai was tired, tired of thinking, but he did not regret his walk back to the deserted village through forests silent and expectant, bathing in streams alone and pensive. It was his leave-taking, and as he stood near the graves, solitary and small, he let his tears go, at first quietly, but then loudly as he wailed into the silence that was to grow even more profound, and last forever once they left.

He stayed there through the short night, not sleeping but simply feeling, absorbing these last impressions of what is, was, and what had come from so far in the past. At dawn as the two suns appeared, the one now a dying hulk spinning helplessly around his rogue world, he rose, sang, prayed, and placed his hand first upon his father's grave, then his mother's, and then the still dark dirt of the more recent mound of his uncle. His hand told him there was still a presence there, lurking, a sentience that had not yet reconciled itself into dust. He could imagine old Luther's words to him as clearly as if the man stood next to him speaking, blowing puffs of mist into the dawn air. He scooped a little dirt from each grave into the leather pouch, the sight of the soil in his hand echoing the dream he had long ago.

He turned his back on that small plot of his small and known world, that remnant of his being, and came away wondering how intertwined place and being really were.

It had helped, this trip into the past, but it did not totally remove the sensations that had drawn him there. Now, back in the city with his family, the future was looming on the horizon. Tomorrow, as they left this world for another, they would also leave behind who they were, who they had become. Never to return. And this is the legacy of their ancestors: to live in constant concern for who they could become.

Would they still care for one another in their new home?

Ursla giggled from the far end of the pool and Antje squealed as her mother swam slowly toward her, only eyes and forehead above the surface, approaching like a sinister parody of a primal water monster bent on devouring her. The young girl's delight was cut short as Ursla found her frail legs flailing for balance, and jerked her under. They both came up sputtering, coughing and choking on laughter as much as the water itself. That's when Ursla spotted him. In her brief, searching and private look, Kai read all the questions, concerns, misgivings. But then he rose, dropping his clothes as he approached the pool.

"Daddy! Daddy! You're back. Come on." She ducked under the water as Kai stepped into the pool, slowly sinking into its giving warmth. Ursla swam over to him and they sat together practically submerged on the low bench along one side. She put her hand on his thigh, and he covered it with his. She kissed him, and then they sat in silence watching Antje's antics.

"It's really O.K., you know. They've been through it a million times. The chambers are all ready to go. The systems are operating perfectly. The computers are programmed. It will work."

"But what will happen to this, our world? And to us?"

Although they had discussed it before, she misunderstood his concern and his question. "We're not certain. We imagine it keeps going until the gravitational devices fail when we leave, so there is the remote chance it will be attracted to our new sun, perhaps our new world. There is a group that wants that to happen, so that it's near us, just in case. Others worry that it might upset the balance of the new world, so I don't know what will happen. That's why we need to leave at the earliest possible second that gravity will allow."

"When did this debate come up?"

"While you were gone. But I guess some of them have been considering the possibilities since the very first, since the record was first deciphered."

"Hmmm. They are always looking for something, aren't they? Does it make any difference, either way?"

"I don't know. No one does."

"It would be a pity to let The Committee have its way after all this time, all these generations. Have we learned anything? Does this group want to remain here, while we go down?"

"I think that is their plan."

"Some things never change. Who will decide? The Council?"

She nodded and they sat in silence as the counterfeit sun dimmed for the last time. The stars began to appear one at a time and Kai watched, after all these years still in wonder at their ingenuity. The night before, he had watched the real stars from the village, far from the city buried in the mountain, that had inspired this art, and realized that this display was already imprinted on him from these, the reflected images, and his own idea of himself had begun a subtle metamorphosis. They had written the star map on the city's night sky, telling the unborn generations what to look for outside, when the time was right and the journey completed. For the first time in his experience, his world was a fixed point in a relationship to the cosmos that was of massive expanse, and that point had purpose and history.

"What I meant was, what is going to happen to us? Are we going to change?" He thought back to that vast plain in his vision, its openness and wide expanse, and wondered what it would require of them.

She looked deeply into him, and squeezed his thigh. "We are always changing."

He took his hand from hers and slid his arm around her waist, stroking her rounded belly. Here, his son was taking form; he knew it. On the far side of the pool, Antje had discovered a bug on the rim and was absorbed in watching its actions. His children, and his lover. A surge of good, warm impulse spread outward, and he knew they would go on. They were his people, and they cared for one another.

# Epilogue

He was coming to and the men hushed. Slowly forcing himself up from the earth, he looked dazed and confused at first, and then, as his vision cleared and a dim recollection began to dawn, he recognized where he was, who was with him, and why. The firelight danced around them, always changing, never quite the same, always varied. The boy looked from face to face around the fire, his anxiety obvious, but also his ability to control it apparent. The old man noted this, before he began.

"Things change. It has always been so. And we change with them." He shifted slightly in his place before continuing. His age required this of him; old bones did not conform easily to the hard earth. But, he had been through this too often not to learn when to move and when to remain dramatically still during the stories. Things like this counted later on when people grew up and made decisions of their own.

First, he told the story of a distant world in the sky where their ancestors had power beyond belief, the story never told outside the clan. The boy's eyes grew as wide as his wonder. After that, they sang, the drum throbbing into the shadows of the tight, round lodge.

Then he told of how they created a world, a moving

world, and the journey they had made across the stars. It was a great epic, full of love and death, villains and heroic actions. He painted that world above in great detail, and dropped into it the horrors of disease and catastrophe with such skill the boy's heart rose and fell on the tones of his voice, the evocative power of his words.

And he told of an old man's vision, of a boy who shared it and cared enough to act, and of his vision and of a woman who grew to fill her times. His telling had the swell of the ocean beneath it, the great vast sea pulsing outside their small camp, and it went long into the night.

At last, dawn approached and they sang to the approaching sun. The old man rose to stretch his tired back as the boy looked into the heart of the fire, reading the past in its light fancy. It was not easy, any more, for the young to make their passage into adulthood. This world was big, and hard, and beautiful. It does not have the minds of people in its mechanisms, but perhaps, that makes it all the better. The voice hummed. He resumed his seat once more, for the final episode.

"And so they prepared, that morning, to come down to this world from the stars: the man, the woman, their child and their people. But things did not go well. Some evil men who intended to make themselves powerful and lead the people from above, stayed behind secretly. They worked magic to try to bond their old world to the new. They worked their magic so they could sit up there pointing to the stars and make the people down here do as they demanded.

"Unfortunately for them, their magic worked, and such is the mystery of things. This new world grabbed the old and it would not let go. Like a dog with a small animal, it shook it and spun it around. It made it spin backwards, as a ball that rolls up hill must stop, then roll backwards on its way down. Everything there was destroyed and, as if fighting back, the old world hurled its sun at this new one. It hit and caused huge fires and destroyed whole races of animals. But, it was too puny to hurt much. Our earth grabbed that rogue world and holds it still, so that we can remember. That is how the moon came to be. The face on it is the face of our people.

"Our people arrived here on it. That is how we came to be. But as the moon and earth fought, the people suffered. Not only those evil ones who died because of their lust for power, but those who wanted only peace. Some never made it down here. They are up there, in the stars, and may return some day to us. Others fell too fast, and crashed here. Still others, we don't know about. They are lost and we search for them. The earth is so large that we have found no trace of them, like we did the others who fell too fast. When we do, we will either rejoice, or bury the dead and mourn them. That is how we are, you see. We care for one another. That is why we roam around, looking for our lost kin."

They sang again, and this time the tune was heavy with an odd mixture of remorse, resignation, hope and pride. It struck to the heart, yet had no words.

He noticed the boy's glassy eyes and knew the time had come. The fasting, the prayers, the proximity of his people and their stories and songs were having their effect. The time had come to leave the boy alone and let the magic work in his imagination.

"That is how our people nearly destroyed themselves, and traveled through oblivion only to be saved by this world of beauty and life. So always respect it for what it has done for us."

He rose unsteadily to his feet, his bones screaming their complaints. "Now, nephew, sleep. Dream. And in the morning we will talk again." The boy looked up at him as if seeing him for the very first time, although he had known him and seen him daily for his whole short life. But now, he was no longer just an uncle; he was a man of power who knew the stories of the deep distant past and the secrets of the universe that they held. He was a man to appreciate.

"Good night uncle."

"Good dreams, my son."

Kai hobbled toward the door. The leg he broke so long ago as they fell onto this new world had never quite healed as it should have. Now, it was a constant reminder, a dull memory as it rose and fell to the earth calling attention to each new step.

He climbed out into the dawn air with a sigh of relief. The ocean lay in the background, but above, on the rise of the land, the great plateau, and beyond it the plain. He had not seen it yet, but he had heard the reports of the scouts who moved in front of the people as they traveled, and he knew he had seen it before, long ago in a dream. "Home," the voice said. He was going home.

Long ago he had marveled at the merging of the voices into one, the Crier's lasting legacy. He knew the boy he had just left and his generation would rise to the tasks they would face. It was always so. And he also knew, with a dull certainty mixed with remorse and understanding, that with it, his story had found its end.